Romance, Rivals and

©Nancy Barone

Also by Nancy Barone

The Husband Diet

My Big Fat Italian Break-Up

Desserted In Sicily

Timeless

The Sicilian Lovers series (coming soon)

To Nick with love

*

To my amazingly talented friend, author Elizabeth Jennings, for her sparkly sprinkles of magic dust...

TABLE OF CONTENTS

CHAPTER ONE: Italian Playboys

CHAPTER TWO: The End

CHAPTER THREE: Mission Impossible

CHAPTER FOUR: A Family Affair

CHAPTER FIVE: Taking the Plunge

CHAPTER SIX: Hysterosalpingography Hysteria

CHAPTER SEVEN: The Home-wrecker Calleth

CHAPTER EIGHT: The Home-wrecker Cometh

CHAPTER NINE: Genie Stacie's Stay

CHAPTER TEN: Goodnight Vienna

CHAPTER ELEVEN: Secret Loves and Love Secrets

CHAPTER TWELVE: Underwear and Understatements

CHAPTER THIRTEEN: Poisonous Love

CHAPTER FOURTEEN: Facing the Facts

CHAPTER FIFTEEN: Jealousy

CHAPTER SIXTEEN: Stefania and Melania

CHAPTER SEVENTEEN: Agony Aunt

CHAPTER EIGHTEEN: Joey

CHAPTER NINETEEN: Fourth and Final Attempt

CHAPTER TWENTY: Family Strangers

CHAPTER TWENTY-ONE: Going Global

CHAPTER ONE: Italian Playboys

Castellino, Tuscany.

"*Ciao, bella*, want arrride?"

I ignored the slowing Ferrari that had materialized next to me on the deserted country road leading from the medieval town of Castellino and trudged my way up the hill to our farmhouse, dragging my flat-wheeled bicycle along.

What was it with this guy? At least a couple of times a year he tried it on and couldn't take *No* for an answer. I was probably the only married woman in the province who hadn't slept with him.

The last thing I needed was to be ambushed by Leonardo Cortini, the local hunk- or so the entire female population thought- who catered to the needs of lonely and/ or bored women down in the Val d'Orcia. Personally, I was neither, so I couldn't understand why he was wasting a single moment of his time with me.

Even when I was a young, love-starved girl in Boston I'd have steered clear from this guy whose ego was the size of a cathedral and who thought he was the best thing in Tuscany since Chianti wine.

Not to brag, but if you were married to the gorgeous former baseball star Julian Foxham, subsequently my kids' principal and now full-time novelist, Leonardo wouldn't be your type either. And I, Erica Cantelli, a forty-three year-old housewife who was always battling to keep the pounds off, was nowhere near Leonardo's type. Nor my hunky husband's, I would soon find out.

Which is why I still had no idea why the Tuscan playboy wanted to play with me on this warm, perfect, early-summer afternoon among the impossibly romantic and picturesque Tuscan hills dotted with cypresses and olive groves. I wasn't warm, nor romantic (maybe a little picturesque) nor Tuscan. So why was he even looking my way?

"Come on, I give you arrride, Eri-ha..." he drawled (Tuscans don't have much use for the 'k' sound) as he came to a full stop, blocking my path.

I bared my teeth at him (old habits die hard) and shook my head, pushing my stubborn handle bars as if they were the ears of a donkey that refused to budge. He laughed, and I threw him my famous hairy eyeball, but he didn't seem fazed.

"So yourrr 'usband's out of town again, *sì?*"

It was the *again* that annoyed me, otherwise I wouldn't have given him the time of day, or be suddenly defensive about the fact that, yes, Julian *was* out of town again to meet his agent Terry Peterson in New York.

They were apparently planning the longest book tour in history. Both Julian's reader fans and baseball fans were waiting with bated breath but I, his wife of seven years, was allowed nowhere near the book- or even his study, for that matter, until it was finished.

That was the only thing I didn't like about Julian being a writer. And the fact that his attention was now divided between our home and rental business in Tuscany and his personal career in the States. To him running *A Taste of Tuscany* was slowly becoming, I could sense it, secondary. Not that he ever refused to collaborate or anything, but he was away a lot of the time, and although it had started out as *my* dream, I always hoped it could be his, too.

But, day by day, he'd carved his own parallel life outside our family routine, delegating his own chores on the property to our co-workers while concentrating more and more on his own craft. Which was his right, of course. But why did that make me feel he cared less and less about A Taste of Tuscany- and us?

"Ah, Ameri-han men- no passion and verrry ambitious!" Leonardo concluded for me. "Eri-ha, be *my* woman and I treat you like a queen!"

Which I found very hard to believe, judging by his reputation. Leonardo Cortini lured the ladies, 'loved' them (as much as a misogynist could) and then left them hanging for all the time it took to make yet another full lap of the female population inhabiting the entire province of Siena, from the Val d'Orcia to Le Crete.

Where else was he going to go? Because Leonardo Cortini had never, get this, been abroad. With all his money and his fast cars, he never actually *travelled* anywhere.

Can you imagine actually sitting home and waiting for someone like that to call you on a Friday night? Come to think of it, that was beginning to sound like *my* relationship with Julian, minus, I hoped, the other women. Only thing was that I never used to sit and wait, always being too busy. But now that the kids were older and the company practically ran itself, it seemed to me I had more time for... well, *by* myself.

But in fairness Julian had never ever given me reason to doubt him (so all we naïve wives say) but after all these years I still found it hard to believe that, in Julian's loving eyes, my personality compensated for my looks.

And because I knew lots of women who had their claws into married men, I kept a close eye on my guy.

You wouldn't believe the stuff I had to put up with even in broad daylight. An endless stream of females (and that's a mouthful for a barely 5k population) parading themselves for Julian's benefit at the market, on Parents' Night or even in the Piazza during our Sunday morning cappuccino. Even the waiter at our favorite café gave him the coy smile. From the morning when we went into town to run our errands, be it to get fresh milk (we had chickens for eggs but as far as farm animals were concerned I drew the line at horses) to our week-end strolls through the streets of Castellino or Cortona or Anghiari, my absolute favorite town in the world, we were always admired. Well, he was admired and I was envied. Hell, were we still *that* odd a couple?

Okay, I know he's a heart-stopper, but, are there no other good-looking men available that they have to prey on mine? I worked hard to find him, ladies. Go get your own. It was like people sensed my *barely-hanging in-there-confidence* and enjoyed making me uncomfortable.

Like this Italian idiot following me home now, getting a clear, unobstructed view of my over-sized derrière.

"My husband will be back very soon," I bit off as Leonardo got out of his car, now towering over me. He sure was good-looking in a savage, but worldly kind of way. The kind of looks that come from money and confidence. And, alas, regular visits to tanning salons.

"Come home with me for *aperitivi*. I make you fantastic *bruschette!* And then, we'll see what happens, *sì?*" said the Big Bad Wolf to not-so-little old me as he hefted my bike out of my hands with a sudden yank. If this was his seduction technique, I wondered how he managed to pull anything more than a muscle. Again I gave him my world-famous hairy eyeball.

"Uh, no, thanks."

That's when, smiling his expensive, fake-tanned smile, he put his hand on my arm. And I realized we were in the middle of the infinite countryside, where no cars or tractors had any business at this time of the year. The wheat was still maturing in the fields, swaying green over hill and dale, and so were the olives in the vast groves, and even the grapes still clung to their vines. Nothing was ready to be reaped, much less me.

In the golden rays of the sinking sun, and the russet reflections reverberating from the fields, I looked at him and, despite my big body, trembled with apprehension. He was much stronger than I. I swallowed, trying to gauge the seriousness of his intentions by the glint in his eye. It wasn't looking good.

"Come on, Eri-ha," he whispered, running his index finger up my arm. "I trrreat you verrry good."

"She already *has* someone treating her good," came my neighbor's voice, Thank you God, from out of the blue. Marco, big, tall, cute in a very boyish, wholesome way, and as good as gold. I sagged in relief, so deep had my terror been I hadn't heard him coming.

Marco and his wife Renata lived a mile down the road and had adopted us from Day One when we had arrived totally clueless and with a container full of dreams. He stepped out of his faded blue *Fiat Nuova Strada* pickup, his fists clenching at his sides, raring to sock Leonardo one or two, although Marco had never, in the eight years I'd known him, hurt a fly.

"She has her family and friends. You are neither. Get lost."

"*Calmati, mi-ha te la mangio,* Calm down, I won't eat her," Leonardo said and Marco turned to snarl at him as he loaded my bike onto his pick-up.

And all this because I'd gone into town after a sudden hankering for a piece of ready-made *panforte* and was too lazy to make it myself. This wasn't the first time my gluttony had got me into trouble. Next time I was taking the Jeep.

Leonardo waved as Marco and I took off with a screech. *"Ciao, Eri-ha, s*ee you soon!"

Not if I could help it.

"If you care about your marriage, stay away from that *pezzo di merda*. He's only trouble," Marco growled as the pick-up ploughed through the colorful countryside still tinged with the golden light of the setting sun. It *was* beautiful.

If only Julian had been there to see it. But at the moment Julian was very far from all this. I decided I wasn't going to tell him about Leonardo. He'd have a fit and probably go down to his house near the river and sock him. He was like that, Julian.

Protective and territorial from the start, when my ex-husband Ira was constantly on my tracks and Julian always alert.

"He sure *looks* like trouble," I said. "Is there any truth to his reputation? That he attacked a woman?"

Marco gave me a sidelong glance and my suspicions were confirmed. "Yes. And he and Renata were officially engaged many years ago."

"Ah."

"*Ah* is right. He left her waiting at the altar, the *bastardo*."

"Now I understand why you hate him."

"Everybody hates him."

"I wonder why he doesn't move away then?"

Again Marco cast me a sidelong glance as we reached the bottom of the hill where my driveway began, looking like a squiggly, drunk's doodle more than a road, with giant, deep green cypresses piercing the now magenta sky as sentinels on the side. "Because he owns half the town, that's why."

I looked over at Marco's face in the rapidly darkening sky. *"Owns?"*

"Yes. The *villa comunale*? He owns that, gardens and all. The secondary school building? His family owns that, too. The public library? They pay rent to *him*. The list is endless- the banks, the post office and all the buildings around the town square. Why do you think it's called Piazza Cortini?"

"Jesus." Eight years and I hadn't made the connection.

"Every medieval building you see has the Cortini coat of arms on it."

"What, the one with the hawk and lilies with the chipped eggs?" To me two white spheres below the hawk looked like eggs, but obviously my mind wasn't as filthy as someone else's who spray-painted a penis in on every single plate bearing the coat of arms. The perpetrator, someone who obviously hated the family, was on a mission.

After the phallus addendum had been dutifully (and quickly) whited out, said perpetrator decided to do a more thorough job and chip off the balls completely.

"They were very intimate with the Medici family centuries ago. He is the only heir to the Cortini dynasty, one of the oldest and richest families in the Val d'Orcia," Marco said as he negotiated the twists and turns up the hill.

"Wow."

"Half the Val d'Orcia is in the hands of a *stronzo*."

I got the message. *Stronzo* is the word I'd have used to describe my ex-husband Ira through and through. (And still do whenever my mind -rarely- strays that way.)

"Didn't you mention to Renata you're on your own tonight?" Marco asked me and I nodded. What else was new?

"Maddy's sleeping over at Angelica's and Warren stayed at uni this weekend."

Which was true for every weekend lately. Normally Warren would return from his flat in Uni, loaded with his laundry and empty Tupperware food containers that I dutifully filled up for him every week, like a good Italian *Mamma*. And when he did come back, he spent all his time with his girlfriend and study-buddy Stefania, although how much studying they get done is debatable.

Rumor had it she actually had her own place, like everyone else, but Warren's was way nicer, so she had decided to sublet hers and sponge off Warren. I mean off us. And now they hardly ever came back to Castellino. I guess they preferred Siena, which was, at least by Italian standards, a larger city.

Maddy and her BFF Angelica, on the other hand, were always holed up in her room or at Angelica's house near the piazza. And the rare times Maddy was at home she'd chat with Angelica on her cell phone. So you see how I'm your typical mother of two who can't get a word out of hrr kids. Which is normal and temporary, they say.

"Mum, get yourself a life and stop badgering me," she'd say when I got too interested in her whereabouts.

15

"Where the hell did she get her temper from?" I'd ask myself loud enough for Julian to hear, hoping he'd have an answer.

He'd step into the kitchen, smile at me and in his good old liverpudlian accent reply, "I haven't the faintest idea, love."

I always told myself Marcy was to blame, taking it out on my dead mother's twin who had passed herself off as my mom for twenty-one years, leaving me in the dark as to why she preferred my siblings Judy and Vince, her biological children.

Once that mystery had been solved, my life had improved overnight. Well, sort of. I was still me, unfortunately. It was Maddy that had taken after Marcy. If on one hand it pissed me off that Marcy's uncontrolled narcissism had rubbed off on my daughter, on the other I was grateful that my own painful, gut-wrenching insecurity didn't penetrate my daughter's soul.

Julian says I spoil the kids rotten, but he's worse than me. When they're late, it's Julian that does all the pacing, the checking of our cell-phones to make sure we've got a proper signal. You'd think he really was their father instead of their (albeit very zealous) ex-principal turned step-father. Legally, they were Foxhams because after our marriage seven years ago Julian had adopted them, much to Ira's indifference.

"Erica?" Marco said, jolting me out of my family musings. "Why don't you come over to dinner tonight? Renata has a pheasant in the oven and our kids haven't seen you forever."

Renata and Marco had helped us start our business and were happy to watch us grow, always at hand in case we needed them. And grow we did, thanks to my business savvy and Julian's contacts. We'd also had some major celebrities from the sports world and even Hollywood, all friends of Julian from his previous life.

Our home was built in local stone and had two stories, a paddock, two swimming pools (one for us and one for the guests) and a tennis court. With his own money and before we married, Julian had separately bought the adjoining acres and the four ruins which we had painstakingly renovated, respecting the Tuscan style and rented out under the name of A Taste of Tuscany to jet-setters from around the world.

Me, I preferred real people like Renata. She and I were very similar, only she is amazing. She runs the family *agriturismo*, a restaurant where they grow their own livestock and vegetables which they serve on a delicious menu. She is a wonderful cook and has taught me loads of recipes while I taught her how to make cheesecake and some Sicilian recipes like *arancini*, these big, sinfully tasty rice balls filled with meat. Just thinking about them made my mouth water. She easily has the best food in the province of Siena and I always recommend her restaurant to my guests.

Which was why I was tempted to go and spend my otherwise empty evening with them.

"I don't know," I said. "I'm not really up to it. I think I'll catch up on my sleep."

"Come on, Eri-ha. It'll be a relaxing evening. Some good Chianti, some *sugo alla lepre-*"

"You had me at the pheasant," I said with a grin. "Ok, I'm in."

He dropped me and my bike off at my front door and I turned to wave.

"I'll stop by tomorrow to fix that," he called as he pulled out.

"Oh, thanks but that's ok. Julian will be home tomorrow."

Marco smiled and drove off. What a wholesome guy. I wondered how Renata could have ever been in love with such a *stronzo* like Leonardo.

CHAPTER TWO: The End

I was piling my freshly-baked muffins into my favorite food-traveler basket, our eight year-old Jack Russell Susie slack-jawed in the hope of a crumb or two, when Maddy and Angelica sauntered in and reached for the goods.

"No more than one each. These are for Renata. There's some cake in the pantry if you want," I said, so proud to be able to say that I'd had time to bake. Ever since we'd upped sticks from Boston our life had literally slowed down. No more rushing down the highway to work, no more speeding tickets, no more feeling sorry for a bad marriage I literally ran from (well, ok- Ira ran. I simply let him).

"Are you going out?" Maddy asked me, surprised as she downed the last of her milk. I had to admit I didn't go out much without Julian. We were always used to doing things together. Was that a bad sign?

"I was going over to dinner at Renata's as you said you were sleeping over at Angelica's, but if you've changed your mind, I'd much rather stay in with you two."

They eyed each other and Maddy said, "Uh, no thanks. Angelica's mom's like, due any minute."

"Oh? Ok, then. Don't forget your keys."

She rolled her eyes. "When have I ever forgotten my keys?"

"Got your toothbrush?"

"Yes," she huffed.

"Right. Well, call me when you need a ride back tomorrow. And say hi to your mom for me Angelica, will you?"

"Sure. Bye, Mrs. Foxham," Angelica smiled sweetly as I turned to go down into the cellar to retrieve a crate of our own wine.

Vino della Tenuta Cantelli, the labels on the bottles read. Can you believe it? If years ago while sipping Chianti with Ira in Boston and talking Tuscany, someone had told me I'd have a vineyard bearing my name I'd have laughed. I looked around our house with great satisfaction. The ceilings featured wooden beams and vaults made up of a myriad of tiny, hand-made terracotta bricks. The floors were original sienna-colored cotto as well, and the furniture was all period antiques.

It had then been a no-brainer leaving my job as hotel manager of the luxurious Farthington Hotel in Boston. When cheating and IRS-scamming husband Ira ditched me, I took Maddy and Warren to Castellino. I had drummed up the nerve to ask Julian to come with us, despite the fact that I'd turned down his first marriage proposal with the promise that I'd consider it while we lived together in sin for the first year. It didn't take me long to stop being afraid and succumb to my dreams. We married in June, two days before his thirty-ninth birthday.

Everything- Julian and the move- had happened all so suddenly, when the bad days had been piling up faster than I could count them and the only friendly face was his- my kids' gorgeous and incredibly kind principal.

I stopped at Maddy's bedroom door that was open for once. Because the walls were frescoed, posters were prohibited, so she had a cork board propped up on her desk, just like Julian had for his writing ideas, only hers was plastered with images she had taken of herself, lips pursed, eyebrow cocked (that was one thing she got from me) and hair tousled.

Yes, she was a beauty. And she was always studying herself in the mirror, so absorbed in her reflection she wouldn't even notice me coming in with her laundry basket. All I could do was hope that it would soon pass, as my Nana Silvia had hoped while watching her own daughter Marcy preen in the mirror, and that it wasn't indeed genetic because otherwise we were screwed for life. At almost sixteen, Maddy represented my biggest headache.

The fear that she'd turn out like her grandmother had driven us to be extra careful and strict, as she was very popular and overly confident of her looks and artistic aptitude. At least that was the message she was sending out. Only I knew that deep down inside

Angelica's mature beauty made Maddy feel like a little girl. Angelica had a shapelier figure, a throaty laugh and that look in her eyes that Maddy, who was at least a year behind in the curves department, didn't have yet.

One day she wanted to be a fashion designer. The next she wanted to be a model slash actress and the third day she wanted to do volunteer work for the orphans in Africa.

"What am I going to do with that girl?" I'd asked myself, hoping Julian would give me an answer.

And now Maddy was almost sixteen and Warren almost twenty. Which made me bloody old. Not that I minded, but when I saw the younger ladies flirting with Julian (who is forty-six next month but doesn't look a day over thirty-six, which means he still looks at least seven years younger than me).

I wished I was twenty again. But then I'd remember what my life was like at twenty, if you could call it a life, practically dragging my blubber along through the years.

I was relieved to be here in Tuscany with the kids, far away from Marcy and my sister Judy who visited every year which was fine with me as long as they didn't stay more than a couple of weeks, time during which they both brainwashed Maddy- not that she needed any persuasion- about the latest trends in make-up, couture and hair.

Warren, on the other hand, was passionately in love with his Stefania, whose mother once told me she couldn't think of a better future husband for her daughter, which made my alarm bells ring every time he brought her home to stay with us.

I was not Stefania's biggest fan, simply because she was a real kiss-ass. In front of the family she would listen enthusiastically and nod her head to our conversations, saying, "I absolutely agree with you, Mrs. Foxham", or, "You are so right, Mrs. Foxham", until you just wanted to smack that smile off her face.

But whenever Warren and I got a moment to catch up on things (we rarely saw each other one on one or even in the family context without Stefania anymore), she would knock and come in before I could stop her, only to stand there and shake her head at him as if saying, *You're not actually listening to your mother, are you?*

Just so we're clear here: I'm happy my son is in love, but it pisses me off to see the way his very *will* is nullified by her mere presence. I'd like my son to mature and go off into the world, but with a brain of his own, not Stefania's.

And then behind my back (I know because Maddy heard her once) she'd say to Warren, "Your mother's an overbearing control freak."

So? I was controlling *my* household, not hers. Unless she was considering taking over for me?

Once she came into the kitchen while I was giving Maddy a piece of my mind and actually stood by my side, folded her arms like me and glared at Maddy as if she was majorly disappointed that her mothering skills hadn't sunk into my daughter's brain.

Maybe Stefania thought I was a helpless, brainless twit like her own mother whom everyone hates (her kids included) but to this day no one has ever told off. Her name is Melania (I remember because it rhymes with Stefania) and she had four kids when she was very young, realized she couldn't cope with them and started blaming their father who was always at work trying to raise the money to feed them. The fact that he could get away from her screeching voice was just a bonus. Mealtimes in that house were a nightmare, not to mention homework time or bath time or any other time.

Melania was so inept (I can't think of a better word to describe her) that she always ferried the kids off to a friend's house in the hope they would help her take care of them. Needless to say her so-called friends would soon tire of her and ditch her, and Melania would have to move on to a new friend. She was cheerful and cute enough to attract people, but soon it would become evident that she was a real loser.

That sounds cruel. Ok, let me put it this way. The truth is that Melania wasn't all there in the brain department. She couldn't keep a job, nor a clean house, nor her own kids. She kept changing religion- and therefore her so-called friends- every change of season. She was imbalanced, unfocused and flaky. She would drag the kids to temple, or The Tent, or the Pagoda-whichever religion seemed in vogue at the moment, just so she wouldn't have to head the Home Affairs Department inside her own apartment. And whenever confronted, Melania, frustrated and incapable of an adult-level of thought or communication, would use her middle finger as a sign that the conversation was over.

Rumors had it she had become a steady drinker and always delegated someone else to pick her kids up (it had even happened to me six or seven years ago) as she was already floored by five o'clock. Now you see, *that* was the kind of wife my ex-husband *Ira* had deserved. Not conscientious, over-anxious, overweight, underestimated *me*.

Neither was Stefania really anything to write home about. To me she looked like a younger version of her mother. Yet Warren was smitten because she always told him what to do. Go figure. When I tried that all I'd get from him was a grunt. Then Stefania would walk in and he'd rise as if magically levitating, his eyes filled with the divine light of her beauty. Love *did* work in mysterious ways.

At the moment Maddy didn't have a boyfriend (so I'm told) at the *Liceo Artistico*, i.e., the art school in Castellino, or anywhere else, but a posse of guys from other schools were constantly texting her and trying to impress her. She got dozens of Whatsapp messages every hour, and her SMS inbox was crammed with all sorts of messages inviting her out on a date. But Maddy just said, "Have you seen his teeth? Ewh!" or, "Oh my

God he's, like, such a junkie!" But to my knowledge she doted on- nor dated, that was the rule for now, no one in particular.

Julian was the same old Julian. Nothing short of a bomb falling onto our house could shake him. He was patient, spoke in his usual low voice, and was never too busy to chat things over with the kids or myself. After one year of living together and seven years of marriage, Julian had proven to be my rock. So when he'd sauntered into the kitchen one morning announcing he wanted to seriously kick-start his writing career we were all thrilled. And now it was becoming apparent he wanted his former fame. *With a vengeance.*

"You can hardly blame the guy. A hunk like that cooped up on a *farm*?" my sister Judy would always say during one of our intercontinental chats at one a.m. She had no idea of what time zones were and regularly called at one a.m, just as I was dreaming my next culinary masterpiece recipe. Which was a huge improvement, considering that in Boston I used to lie awake thinking of how to kill Ira and get away with it.

Judy always tended to exaggerate, of course. But lately I had to admit Julian looked as if he *needed* more than just us in his life. I wondered what it was. Julian loved living in Tuscany, or rather, coming *back* to it as he was hardly ever in the country. I wondered if he was still happy as the day we'd moved here. Was he still happy with me as I was with him?

Was I the only one who hadn't changed? For sure I wasn't as stressed as my Boston days. I loved living here. I had everything I could possibly want- my own business, a beautiful house, good friends and a fantastic family. But (there's always one but too many, and in this case I'd soon find out it was all about one *butt* too many) deep down I felt something was missing, too.

*

I drove home from Renata's late that evening in a squiggly if not drunken line (there was only a narrow dirt road leading back home so no risk in running anybody over or smashing into a telephone pole) and parked my red Citroen Picasso outside the front. Julian was due in time for breakfast and the kids not until the next day at dinnertime. Funny how life revolved around food in Tuscany.

Tuscany. I'd finally made it, after years of pining and dreaming and surfing the net for a good deal (that doesn't exist unless you're filthy rich, by the way). After it had become apparent that Ira wasn't willing to leave the States but before it became clear that he was leaving us, I'd actually given up on my dream of moving here. To tell the truth, I'd given up on lots of things. I'd let go of myself, my dreams of love and self-realization.

And after I'd left Little Italy, where I'd been happy only in the presence of my Nonna Silvia and my Aunts Maria, Martina and Monica, I had found happiness here with Julian.

Castellino was a great place to live. It had everything- great weather, magnificent culture, amazing food and wine, monuments and churches- and an amazing countryside. And most of all, beautiful, friendly people who went out of their way to help you. There was only one thing.

Everybody knew everybody else's business, especially who is divorcing whom. Many of Maddy's and Warren's friends' parents were separating or legally divorced, or simply seeing someone else on the side in what they believed to be total secrecy. How did they expect their affairs to be private in a village where the baker puts more bread and possibly a cake aside for you because he's heard you're going to have people over for dinner?

But all in all, it was finally a tranquil life and I was grateful for everything.

The telephone rang as I was getting ready for bed. It was one a.m. so it had to be Judy. When I was living in Boston just ten minutes away from her she never wanted to know. Now she was all *Sis here and Sis there*. Go figure.

"Erica?"

"Hey," I said and yawned.

"I won't keep you if you're gonna be like that," she snapped.

"Be like what?" I countered. She had a temper worse than mine.

She huffed. "I can't talk anyway. I'm going on a shopping trip with Marcy."

As long as it wasn't Milan. Every year they did this to me- flew to Milan, called to say they just wanted to swing by (Milan is an hour's flight from here) and ended up staying two weeks. Not that I didn't love them or anything, but if individually they were a handful, together they were deadly. They'd talk fashion twenty-four seven and gossip about all the stars as if they knew them personally. And beg Julian, who did, for tidbits.

"Marcy wants to be there by next week."

"There where?" I asked, a deadly suspicion rising from my stomach to my throat. It couldn't be. Not even Marcy would do that on such short notice.

"At your place. She's finally convinced the whole tribe to come and see you guys. Even Vince and Sandra are coming with Vito and Michael. (Need I mention my brother's obsession with The Godfather, Parts One, Two and Three?) "He checked your website and saw there are no bookings for two weeks."

Two weeks? *Those* two weeks? The ones we always marked as unavailable because that was when we went away? We had already planned a week in Sardinia and one in Sicily. I already had tickets!

"But- but..." I faltered.

"Ah, don't tell me," Judy said. "I'm missing out on two weeks of my gym classes, you know."

If my sister's past was anything to go by, gym class meant everything to her. If she was missing out on two weeks with a possible new trainer/lover, I could miss out on Sicily and Sardinia, according to her twisted logic. I slammed my mouth shut. I didn't want to argue before she even got here. The Cantellis had a way of turning any dinner into a disaster.

"Right. Let me know your arrival details and I'll come pick you guys up at the airport."

"Bring two vans. The aunts are coming as well."

Now *that*, on the contrary, was good news. My aunts Maria, Martina and Monica were loads of fun. Everything went well when they were around. The three of them co-owned a successful restaurant called *Le Tre Donne*, the three women. The fact that Marcy hadn't been invited into the joint venture spoke worlds on its own. Marcy didn't get along with them.

Ever since Marcy married my dad, she became jealous of the attention he was getting from her sisters. Maria was an amazing cook and always brought dinner to us from their apartment downstairs until I was able to do the cooking. And even then they'd stuck around to teach me everything they knew about home-making, which was quite a lot.

Zia Martina was the seamstress, laundress and artist. She would launder dad's shirts and sew him classy suits from the Italian cloth that arrived at my dad's store, Italian Assorted Gifts.

Zia Monica, the youngest, was the computer expert and accountant. The three of them, even long after my *Nonna* had died, had gathered to take care of me, Judy, Vince and my dad, fully aware that Marcy never could and didn't even try.

They were all beautiful, sharp-witted, extremely classy and had a soft spot for Maddy and Warren. They were also crazy about Julian who, I guess in appreciation of all they'd done for me, spoiled them rotten. It would be great to see them again.

Next was my brother Vince, who acted like Vito Corleone, the overbearing, know-it-all husband when he sat at his table, but turned into a little lamb in Marcy's presence. He adored her and treated her like the matriarch of his family, although God knows how he'd come to that conclusion.

His poor wife Sandra, whom he'd fallen out of love with years ago, simply bore with him, presumably because he was a great dad. He loved Vito and Michael.

Judy's husband Steve, a true-blood American guy whom she'd cheated on more times than I could count, had thrown her out once. She'd always been a bit of a floozy, Judy. But her kids, Jake, Jamie and Tony were a great bunch.

Thinking of all the fun things we could do together if Marcy didn't ruin everything at least once a day, I fluffed up my pillow and shifted to my frog-like position when the phone rang again.

"Hello?"

Silence.

"Hello?" I repeated. We had shit connection sometimes.

"Hello, is this that holiday place?" said a woman in an American accent who, if I may add, didn't sound awfully bright.

"Yes, this is A Taste of Tuscany, how may I help you?"

"I need to speak to Julian." No 'May I?', no please.

I cleared my throat. "I'm sorry, Mr. Foxham isn't available at the moment. May I take a message?"

Dead-pan silence.

"Hello? May I ask who's calling, please?"

"Never mind," the voice said. A voice I'd heard before. "I'll call his cell phone." And with that, the line went dead.

Now *you* try to get to sleep after a call like that.

Eventually when I did drop off, but woke up to the sound of the phone again, groaning as my fingers grasped the dreaded thing. I wondered whether that was that American woman again, and how she'd managed to get Julian's cell phone number of which, by the way, he was extremely secretive.

"H'llo?" I rasped. At least I think it was me. Jesus, no more *Chianti* after ten. And no more *Tagliatelle al sugo di lepre*, either. I just couldn't stomach that wild food anymore.

"*Signora Cantelli?*" came an unfamiliar voice. A man, this time, and Italian.

"*Sì?*"

"Mr. Julian Foxham's wife?" the voice persisted.

"Yes?" I sat up, instantly awake. "Who is this?"

"I'm sorry, *Signora*. There's been an accident. *Il Signor* Foxham didn't make it to the hospital. I'm sorry."

I reached out, feeling for Julian's warm body, but the bed was empty. But that was ok because he wasn't supposed to be back until the morning.

"You're dreaming. Wake up," I said to myself. "It's just a stupid prank. Come on, wake up, dammit!"

"*Signora* Cantelli?" continued the voice. "I'm sending you a squad car."

To identify the body. Oh my God. "Where... did it happen?"

"Just outside Cortona..."

Cortona? "Impossible. He's away on business..." Apart from the fact that we didn't know anybody in Cortona. Did we?

"He was on his way to see... someone."

"Who?"

"A... friend."

As if it mattered, I tried to think of who the friend could be. But we knew the same people. And then I understood. Julian had a lover, and he had been going to see her. In the middle of the night. So much for his bloody meetings with his agent. So much for the loyal husband bit. Now I understood his restless attitude, his listless behavior. My husband of seven years had finally tired of me and wanted out. Only he'd taken it to extremes, because now, not only was he out, he was *gone*.

"Signora Cantelli?"

"Who is she? Tell me!" I cried, my voice sounding muffled, echo-ey, like I was crying from the bottom of the ocean, and after a confused moment of silence, the line went dead. "Tell me!"

Sweetheart, came a voice from above the ocean, and I flapped my arms as if they were fins, trying to make my way back to the surface. *Wake up, you're having a bad dream.*

I opened my eyes, relieved it was only a nightmare. But it wasn't, because the bed was still empty. I hadn't dreamed it at all. Julian really was dead.

"Julian!" I cried at the top of my lungs, my throat dry and my heart a big black swinging demolition ball in my chest. "Julian, come back!"

"I'm just here, sweetie," came his voice, followed by his beautiful head as it poked around the corner of the en-suite door. He returned with a glass of water and sat down on the bed next to me as I gulped it down in one snap of my neck and threw myself up into his arms, squashing his middle-section, trying to explain. "You had died!" I managed before I broke down into a new fit of tears. "In a car crash on your way to your lover's house!"

Julian put his arms around me and moaned, "Again?" But then his face split into a grin, and it was like the sun had come out in the middle of the night.

"Serves me right then, doesn't it?" he said.

"It's not funny, you know," I argued, trying to shake off the dreadful feeling of tragedy that still clung to me like a pair of soaking pajamas.

"Honey, when are you going to get it through your thick skull that I'm not going anywhere. I'm healthy. I drive very carefully."

"But you *cheated* on me…"

He sighed. "Only in your worst nightmares. But you know I love you and you only. And I wouldn't cheat on you for all the women in the world. Not ever. Okay?"

I nodded fiercely, refusing to let go of him. Boy, if this kept up I'd have to fly my former shrink, Dr. Denholm, over to Tuscany in a jiffy. Maybe even take him up as a permanent resident here at *A Taste of Tuscany*. Shit, was this what my life was becoming? I had a wonderful husband, a loving family, a business that I actually liked. And I never looked and felt healthier. On the *outside*.

But on the inside, it was chaos. My mind was going for a hike every night. But luckily it returned before I woke up in the morning. How did people have such bad dreams and actually manage to keep a hold on sanity?

The truth was that, after seven years of marriage to this wonderful, sexy man, I was so happy I was terrified. All I needed was one glitch and my whole world would cave in. All I needed was one of my loved ones to be in an accident or become ill and good night Vienna. That was our life down the drain. Did I really need all that drama, no, *tragedy,* in my life? What the heck was wrong with me? But seriously- wouldn't it be corny if one day I discovered that Julian *was* bonking the barmaid, the butcher's daughter or even Maddy's art teacher?

For eight years we lived an idyllic life, watching the children grow. I painted, dragged Julian onto my hot air balloon trips, did the laundry for our guests and Julian tended to our horses and wrote his books. We enjoyed good friendships and all was well. It was so well that I started having these nightmares.

I wasn't actually *jealous* of Julian or anything, at least I don't think so. He was a thoughtful, considerate host when we had people over, but never once did I ever get the danger-zone vibe. Never once, despite many women's steady, inviting gazes (yes, in my own house, right in front of me), did I ever get the feeling that he wasn't just being courteous towards them. Yet, I still felt something was missing from our lives.

Smarten up, a demon-voice would say inside me. *Can't you see he's cheating on you, left, right and center? Do you really think that such a good-looking guy is going to stay faithful to you?*

Of course I do, I'd answer the mean voice, and then I'd be okay for a long time.

But you know when you get those foreboding feelings, you positively know some tragedy is going to strike, although you can't quite put your finger on which kind?

Nonsense, I'd reply to myself. *Nothing bad is going to happen. Just shut up and enjoy your life, you lucky idiot.*

My brain was a one-woman band with multiple personalities. One day I'd be so confident about everything and the next I wasn't even sure of my rock-solid skills, like cooking, painting and my business sense).

Julian loves you and that's that, my heart told me. And I really believed he did. Until another woman would land like a bomb on our home (only I didn't know that yet), and my nightmare would come true.

"Erica...?" Julian said.

I looked up, my arms still wrapped tight around him. "Yeah?"

"Can you let go sweetie? I've just got in and I'm breaking my neck for a pee."

"Oh. Sorry."

Just as I was getting back to sleep Julian's cell phone rang. Two a.m.

"Can you get that?" he called from the bathroom. "It's probably Terry- he's worse than your sister with time zones."

I groaned and rolled over to his side of the bed and night table. "Hello?"

Silence.

Now this time I was awake and Julian was here, safe and sound. Unless... Maddy? Warren? Alarm bells started ringing. I expected to hear Angelica's Mom or

Stefania saying something had happened, but no one spoke.

"Hello?" I said, louder, sitting up.

More silence, and then a click.

"Who is it?" Julian asked, taking off his clothes.

I shrugged. "They hung up."

Now if I were a suspicious wife and Julian a sleaze-ball, we'd have a real problem on our hands. But Julian was not the cheating kind. With him, thankfully, I was on safe ground. For once. Or so I thought.

CHAPTER THREE: Mission Impossible

The first thing I felt when I woke up the next morning was a wet, sticky sensation, like the guy in The Godfather who finds his dead horse's head in his bed. Yeah, sorry, that's sick, but it's also *exactly* how I felt. My period, biblically late, had made its appearance with a vengeance. That was my body lately. I'd have dry spells and then, just like that, *woosh*- the Nile would flood. I jumped to my feet, not daring to look back at the mess I'd made of our bed.

"Are you alright?" Julian asked from behind the bathroom door. I quickly washed and emerged, finding him sitting on the bed, wide awake now.

"Sorry- had a little accident. I have to change the sheets."

He looked at me and shook his head before reaching into the linen closet for the burgundy sheets, the ones I always put on the bed during my period. It was kind of a signal that sex was off limits during those days. He knew the code. Burgundy meant no sex. So why was he shaking his head like that?

"Why are you shaking your head like that?"

"I was kind of hoping you weren't going to get it this month."

"That would be cruel if I were on menopause alert," I objected as I billowed the sheets out before me.

"Erica- do I have to spell it out to you? I was hoping you'd get pregnant," he whispered as he caught the sheet and tucked it in on his side. I giggled at his joke, but he didn't join in. Was he serious?

"Are you serious?"

Julian stopped plumping his pillow inside its new case and looked at me with an expression I'd never seen before, and nodded, his eyes studying me.

I swallowed. "Please tell me you're still asleep and sleep-talking, or rather, that I am and this is just a silly dream?"

"No dream, Erica. I'd like a child. Wouldn't you?"

We never discussed this in eight years and he wanted a child *now?* "I'm forty-three, Julian," I said as if apologizing. Apologizing for what, I wondered- not being the automatic baby dispenser that I was while married to Ira?

I let myself fall onto our now burgundy bed with all my weight, which was still quite noticeable. I had gained ten kilos in eight years, and at eighty-five kilos, I was anything but slender. How the heck was I going to face another pregnancy? I looked up and wished I hadn't because Julian was getting down on his knees by the bed, taking my hands and searching my face, like he had eight years ago when trying to convince me we were made for each other.

"Don't say anything, honey. Just promise me you'll give it a thought."

Give it a thought? I was so shocked I couldn't think of anything *else*. Did have have any idea of what he was asking me?

"It'll be great, you'll see. Raising her will be a dream."

"Her?"

He grinned. "I've always wanted a little girl."

"A girl?"

"I'll be just as happy with a boy, of course. And you?"

"I've, uhm, got to go the bathroom again," I said, sliding off the bed. *And possibly slash my wrists.* What planet did my adorable husband live on? I could already picture myself expanding until I resembled the hot air balloon Julian had bought me upon our arrival in Tuscany. He'd made all my dreams come true. Time to return the favor. As if I didn't have enough problems.

*

"How was having Chiara so late in your marriage?" I blurted out to my BFF Renata as we were lunching under my pergola.

She snorted. "Why, are you thinking of having another kid?"

When I didn't answer she almost choked on her *cacciucco*. So I whacked her on the back.

"Oh, God- why didn't you tell me you and Julian were having problems?" she wheezed before gulping down a glass of San Pellegrino water.

I stopped in mid-bite. "What? What are you talking about?"

Renata cleared her throat and stared back at me, her eyes watering.

"A baby at this age is usually a fixer-upper. So what's going on?"

I shrugged, inwardly panicking at the news. Was that why Julian wanted a baby? To fix a problem I wasn't even *aware* of? Impossible. I'd know if there was a problem. Right?

"Nothing's going on. Just... Julian wants one."

"*Oyoy*," Renata sighed. The typical Tuscan, *something is wrong* sigh. "Not good."

"Shut up," I said, cutting away furiously at my *carpaccio* and rocket lettuce. "Julian and I are fine."

"Are you sure?" she insisted, not taking her eyes off me.

I rolled my eyes. "Of course I'm sure."

"Hmmm, I don't know. That's pretty sudden, isn't it? Why don't you ask him?"

"Ask him why he wants a kid? It's obvious."

"He could've had one all this time. Why now?"

My sentiments exactly.

*

"Good thing you live far away in that little peaceful bubble of yours," Judy said to me during our weekly one a.m. chat as I sat on the floor next to the bureau, knees under my chin. One more pound and I wouldn't be able to do that anymore. I know that for a fact because once I'd pigged out at a restaurant and suddenly my stomach was in the way. It had taken me three months of practically fasting before I returned from The Point of No Return, i.e., that two-three pound range beyond which I was once again officially uncomfortable in my own, bursting skin. Boy, had that been close. Not that it wasn't in the way now, but I could still keep it at bay by squishing my thighs up against it and wrapping my arms around my knees. Time to go easy on the Tiramisu.

"So how is living in paradise?" my sister Judy asked, and I pictured her sitting in her kitchen amidst the remains of a family dinner.

"I feel great," I lied, then thought, *what the heck.* "I'm so happy I'm terrified," I whispered.

I heard her exhale. "Why?"

I shrugged, as if she could see me. "I dunno. I just keep waiting for this bomb to drop." There was no way I was telling Judy about Julian's request for a child, not yet, anyway. And it was true- I was terrified. Even during the day I'd catch myself dreading losing it all, either through Julian's abandoning me for another woman, or his death, which would have been, if I'd have any say in it, only minutes apart.

Was our life just too perfect? Nothing bad ever happened. We were living what you'd call a life of domestic bliss. Yet this baby thing really was bugging me.

Judy inhaled deeply and I could almost see the smoke.

"I thought you'd quit smoking, after all you put Steve through," I said, meaning her quasi-divorce over her gym instructor, or, The Face Eater, as I'd dubbed him eight years ago.

Judy exhaled. "Oh, get real," she said. "I learned to cook, didn't I? And that's still one more thing than *Marcy* ever did. Anyway, I'm glad for you that everything is perfect, although I don't believe it ever lasts," Judy sentenced. "Because really all men care about are looks. So keep fit or you'll *lose* him to some skinny floozie."

To hell with anybody's feelings. That was Judy for you- blunt and tactless.

"Actually, Julian and I are trying to get pregnant," I blurted out.

Whoah. Where had *that* come from? I'd told Julian I'd *think* about it. And now my mouth had suddenly decided- without even consulting me- that I wanted me to become a mother- again.

Silence on the other end. I waited, wondering how long it was going to take Judy to enter her usual routine of lectures about keeping a figure. Because, unlike Renata, Judy never questioned the deeper whys and wherefores. She didn't disappoint me, of course.

"Oh, Erica, what the hell *for*?" she gasped, and I could almost see her eyebrows shoot into her hairline with what could only be described as disgust at the thought of a levitating me. "You already have two- why the hell do you want another one?" Judy had three herself, but her second was a twin-birth so she'd got shafted, in her opinion. But if you look at it figure-wise, she only had to get fat twice for three children. It figured, didn't it?

"Erica," Judy continued. "If you were still, say, in your thirties and didn't have any, I'd understand, but I just don't get why you want to put yourself through all that again."

"Uh, because Julian wants a child of his own?" That would have been the perfect moment for any woman to question the reason behind a man's wishes. As per her character, Judy let the moment pass.

"So what?" she said flatly. "Tell him to get a surrogate. You don't want to totally blimp out again, do you?"

Then she gasped. "Did you say yes?"

"Er- not exactly."

"Well put him out of his misery and tell him if he wants a baby to look around somewhere else! You already gave. Unless-"

"Unless what?"

"Are you guys in a rut?"

Oh my God, was it true then? Judy was the man expert. If she confirmed Renata's opinion then it had to be right. We were in a rut and Julian thought that the only way out was having a kid? What ever happened to working on things?

Although we'd been together for over eight years, we had only been married seven so were still technically subject to The Seven Year Itch. The unlucky year in marriages.

True, we hadn't had sex in quite a while because he was hardly ever around. When I'd screwed up in the past, too taken with my new B&B years ago, I'd almost lost him. But we'd promised to put that behind us forever. The kids alone had soaked up three quarters of our marriage when they were younger and-oh. Okay. I think I got it now. I needed to stay focused on my wonderful, fantastic husband. Do more for him. Avoid making the same mistake. Get the sex rolling again.

But the mirror told me I was going to have one helluva time doing *that.* *You* try munching on rice-cakes and lettuce for eight years) and was still very far from looking like Angelina Jolie. But Julian was ten times more handsome than Brad Pitt, and even they hadn't lasted very long.

After eight years, I'd finally understood why he was with me. We *completed* each other, like Tom Cruise said to René Zellweger in Jerry Maguire. We were made for each other. Where he was lacking (Julian was a mega-procrastinator) I prodded him every step of the way, but we both enjoyed it because I'm bossy and he loves it). I filled his gaps, he filled mine. Where *I* was uncertain he was confident and pulled me along.

And he was the perfect step-father. Way better with the kids than Ira had ever been. Maddy and Warren adored him more than ever because he was the hip one, the sporty one and he returned their affection ten-fold. He'd always had time for them. A little less now that he was famous again, though.

He'd already published a couple of novels about the world of baseball years ago and was now writing a novel about the coming of age of a young baseball player and his ascent to stardom. I knew this one was the closest he'd ever get to autobiographical. His agent was begging him for an autobiography, but Julian always shook his head.

In a way, though. he was writing about his first success as a youngster, followed by his own come-back as a mature man.

"I can't even picture Marcy's face when she finds out she's gonna be a grandma again," Judy said with a giggle and I joined her.

"The first thing she'll say will be, *I'm not coming out this summer to babysit!*"

"Thank God. No offense Erica, but I hate coming out there with the whole family. Next time I'm coming on my own. For your baby's birth."

"You're going to have a long wait," I said.

Judy snorted. "I thought so. You tell him."

Tell Julian? I'd have to, because I really wasn't getting good vibes about this baby thing.

CHAPTER FOUR: A Family Affair

They say Italian families are particularly solid, but you wouldn't say that looking at the Cantellis. The whole band, all fourteen of them, came and left, you won't be surprised to hear, in the space of three days. Cause? Marcy's big mouth.

We were having a lazy lunch under the wisteria-laden pergola. Thinking back, I could put it down to the excessive heat, maybe even the Scirocco breeze known to have driven people to murder. But we all knew whose fault it was.

Marcy came up with one of her outrageous but not out of the ordinary comments about my cooking. Dad made the big mistake of snorting and saying something under his breath. I can't remember all the details but it went something like this:

"Edward, what are you muttering about?"

"Nothing, dear."

"Nothing? You've been like this for months now. Will you please tell me why you are never happy?"

Dad stared at her for a long moment before he said, "*I'm* never happy? Jesus Christ, Marcy- if anyone here is always complaining it's you. Just leave your sisters alone. And stop ruining everything."

That alone shocked us all, because dad never raised his voice. He was the mildest man in creation. And Marcy wasn't used to anyone talking back at her.

That earned him a smile but also a silent admonishment from my eldest aunt Maria who could smell trouble a mile off, especially where Marcy was concerned.

"Me?" Marcy said in horror. "You didn't even want to come out here in the first place! I had to drag you!"

Judy snickered while Julian glanced at me but I was too busy closing my eyes and praying Marcy wouldn't be there when I reopened them.

"Okay, Marcy," Julian said softly. Even though she lived on the other side of the ocean her outbursts were legendary even to him. "Come and help me dish up dessert now?"

That's when she turned to me. *Me.* I hadn't even *breathed.* "Dessert? When are you going to understand that I don't eat dessert? How do you think I manage to fit into my clothes, by having dessert after every meal like you?"

I shot a quick glance around the table. Besides Julian, no one seemed to have heard a word. So she continued, in a louder voice. "If you'd only listened to Ira instead of complaining about what a bad husband he was you wouldn't be on your second marriage, with all due respect to Julian here."

"I never complained to you about Ira," I countered, always flammable but still wary of an argument in front of the entire family. "Never. I always kept my problems to myself." And before I could stop myself, I added, "Besides, you'd be the last person I'd talk to."

Marcy looked at me with rounded eyes. "What's that supposed to mean?"

I snorted. "That if it weren't for Nonna Silvia who raised us I'd be a basket case."

"You *are* a basket case!" Marcy assured me. "Look at yourself! You lost Ira because you couldn't take care of him or yourself. He had to blackmail you into surgery so you could fit through the door!"

Julian glanced at me (that was news for him) before he cleared his throat, but Marcy interrupted him. "And now that you're married to a sex symbol who's on all major chat shows you *still* don't take care of yourself! Look at you in that bland green sundress, pony tail and your flip flops. *Flip flops*, where do you think you are, the beach? Do you want to lose him to some Hollywood movie star or something?"

Julian coughed. "Uh, actually, Marcy, I like the way my wife looks very much."

I beamed at him and he squeezed my hand. "Now," he continued. "Who wants dessert?"

There was a collective "Me" as I cleared the dishes, eyeing Marcy who sat back, not even dreaming of helping Maddy and me.

"I hope it's not one of Erica's fat-bomb cakes," she muttered to anyone who would listen.

Maddy was too young and inexperienced in the Cantelli affairs to know any better. "I like Mom's cakes, Nana."

Marcy snorted. "Watch out you don't explode like your mother. And don't call me Nana."

"Why not?" Dad barked and I flinched at the unfamiliar sound of his raised voice. It was like he'd finally found a backbone from under the table. Good for him. "They are your grand-children. You've got seven of them."

"And God knows how many more," Judy added. Everyone, me included, stared at her.

Dead silence. "What's that supposed to mean?" Vince suddenly demanded.

"I don't need to be reminded of my grand-children with all the babysitting I've done in my life-" (At that Judy, Vince, Sandra and I snorted. Steve, who was too polite, and Julian, who hadn't been around early enough back then, sat in silence) "it's a wonder they don't call *me* Mom."

"No one *dares* call you Mom," Judy snapped, then turned to me. "What is it she says?"

"Children belong to their parents, not their grandparents," I answered. I knew the spiel by heart.

"I don't recall *your* mother ever saying that to you when she used to watch them while you slept your afternoons away," Dad said, glaring at Marcy who shot him an injured look. "What? I'm not allowed to say the truth? If it wasn't for poor old Silvia, bless her soul in heaven, and your sisters here, we'd be dead by now."

"Yeah, and what a great job she and my marvelous sisters have done!" Marcy spat. "My eldest daughter's a fat loser, my youngest is a slut who sleeps around (at that Steve turned beet red and excused himself) and my only son has had more affairs than I can count."

Sandra blanched and turned to Vince. "They *know*?" she squeaked.

Vince swallowed and dared a quick glance around the table. "Let's go upstairs, honey. I think I've heard enough."

"But I haven't!" Sandra snapped.

I put my head in my hands again.

"Slut?" Judy cried in disbelief. "At least I didn't abandon my baby!"

I stared at Judy, stupefied. I thought that was a secret Marcy had revealed only to me, in a sign of truce years ago. "You knew?" I asked my sister.

"Of course I knew. You thought you were the bearer of her only secrets? She can't keep a secret any more than she can hold her booze."

"Abandon?" Vince whispered wide-eyed and sitting back down and even Sandra seemed to have forgotten her own little drama. "What's she talking about, Ma?"

"About the fact that your angelic and celestial mother had a baby before she married Dad. In England," Judy sneered. "She left him on the steps of a church, for Christ's sake! Anyone beat that if you can!"

Julian's head snapped up and he stared at Marcy. Really hard. I suppose she would never stop surprising him, or any of us.

My eyes swung to poor old Dad who, sat pale and still. Shit. Everyone seemed to know but him.

"Dad?" I whispered. "Are you ok?"

"Edoardo?" Zia Martina asked, placing her hand on his, which Marcy readily slapped.

Dad didn't flinch but stared ahead for a long time as if he hadn't hear or felt any of it. Or as if he had a gazillion times. I held my breath, waiting for him to say something.

"Dad?" I nudged him gently, my heart skipping a beat.

"Edoardo?" Julian echoed me.

Dad turned to us with a sweet, sweet smile. "Yes? I'm fine, thanks. Marcy, I think you have quite e few apologies to make before you leave this table. Julian, please pour me another glass of that fantastic wine you and my lovely daughter make, would you mind?"

Julian stared at him at length, then nodded, his eyes darting to Marcy.

I took advantage of that beat and left the table for barely thirty seconds, almost missing the Grand Finale. I wish I had.

"She's so bloody obese!"

"Marcy," Julian said. "With all due respect I think you've had too much to drink. Now why don't you go upstairs and lie down for a while?"

"I don't want to lie down," she snarled.

"Of course she doesn't," Judy snapped. "She's been horizontal all her life. And not always alone."

Marcy crossed her arms and glared at her. "Look who's talking, Mother Theresa of Calcutta."

"Yeah, well at least I had the decency of sleeping with guys my age."

"What?" I said. Had my mom had an affair while she was married to my dad as well? And with a younger man?

"Oh, you don't know about her toy-boy?" Judy said as I returned with the dessert tray laden with my home made *Tiramisù, Cantuccini* and *Castagnaccio,* a fresh pot of espresso coffee and some *Vin Santo* for the *Cantuccini.* I could feel my ears getting hot, and I can tell you the situation was getting way too out of hand even for someone as confrontational as me.

"Toy-boy?" I squeaked.

"Yeah," Judy said. "A kid from your school, too."

I froze, my voice struggling out of my mouth. "Who?"

"That cute Italian dropout, remember the one that used to take the older girls behind the supermarket? What was his name? Tony- Tony Esposito."

Not just the older girls. He'd taken me, too, but no one needed to know that.

I turned to Marcy, barely breathing. "You slept with a *kid*?"

"He wasn't a kid. He was eighteen."

"And you were what, forty-something?" I countered, rapidly calculating the age difference.

I looked around at my family, from my parents to my siblings and their families to my aunts to my own children. What a family we were.

Dad and Marcy were at the end of the line, it seemed to me.

Vince and Sandra, ditto.

Judy and Steve, ditto as well.

But as I thanked my lucky stars for my healthy relationship with Julian, I couldn't help but wonder. Were we next? Why was it that hard to stay together? I was one to wonder. Ira had almost driven me to insanity/slash depression. I should be supportive of them, not melancholic. Still, when I look back and remember our childhood, I saw the signs, loud and painful.

My aunts, who had never had boyfriends we know of, seemed to be the only ones that, besides Julian and myself, were happy. How did they manage to be so happy and not be lonely?

"Ok, everybody pipe down now, please and enjoy your desserts. We've had enough drama for today," Julian said. "I suggest you all go to your rooms and calm down for the rest of the afternoon. It's too hot to do anything anyway."

"Marcy- apologize to Erica and Julian," Dad said softly.

"It doesn't matter," I said hastily. I just wanted to get this lunch over without any bloodshed.

"Yes, it does, sweetheart," he assured me. "Marcy?"

But Marcy just glared at him and took another sip of her wine.

"Please," I whispered. "It doesn't matter anymore. I'm okay."

At that point an angry Zia Maria turned to me.

"Of course you are sweetie. Because you are like your mother Emanuela. You've got guts and you are strong. You have all her best traits and she had all of Nonna Silvia's."

Marcy snorted and lifted her empty glass.

"Yeah, Manu was a real concentrate of virtue. She had sex with your dad on their first date."

"Do *not*... even try to soil your sister's reputation," Zia Maria, the most concerned of the family reputation, warned her.

"You shut up!" Marcy slurred. "You frustrated bitch!"

Why, oh why, did my family have to drag their family baggage all the way across the ocean? Couldn't they just bring sunscreen and flipflops like every other traveler? No, of course not, we had to flog every family issue of the last fifty years, from my aunts' role in our lives to my weight, to Judy's infidelity- but never, ever, Marcy's flaws. Normal admin in the Cantelli household.

*

"Thanks for your support, honey," I said to Julian as I loaded the dishwasher.

He shook his head. "Your family never ceases to amaze me."

I snorted. "That was nothing. You should've seen Marcy at Maddy's christening."

"Oh yeah?"

"She climbed up onto the table and accused her sisters of having an affair with my dad- simultaneously. She was drunk as usual, of course."

"Jesus."

"Yeah. I'm going to have to do something about that. It's way out of hand- more than I thought."

"Honey," he said, hugging me. "You are not your mother's keeper. She's an adult and has to learn to take care of herself. Or if not, she has plenty of people to lean on. You live on the other side of the Atlantic and have got your hands full enough as it is, yes?"

I frowned. He was right- I was the least qualified in any case to deal with her, what with our stormy past.

Needless to say Marcy had just shattered three couples including her own marriage in the space of five minutes, and in less than two hours each had boarded a different plane back home. What should've been two weeks of hell was concentrated in three days. One needs to always look for the silver lining.

*

A week later I called my dad's cell phone. "Hey Dad, how are you?"

A long, long sigh. "I swear to you, Erica, your mother is killing me. After forty-three years she still drives me crazy. She's going to die an old selfish woman. And even if she lived to be a hundred years, she will never be like my Manu."

Manu. Emanuela, my real mother whom I've never met. Just the thought of her made me smile. When I didn't burst into tears.

"Dad…" I faltered. This was the very first time I'd ever heard him complain about Marcy. I always thought he was happy to be her slave, valet, etc. How the hell was I supposed to know he was suffering?

He cleared his throat. "Sweetie, I'm sorry. But I've had enough. For years I've put up with your mother and now I know that I'll be spending our next anniversary in jail because I am going to kill her very soon."

One wonders why he hadn't thought of it sooner.

CHAPTER FIVE: Taking the Plunge

On the force of my sister's words, I worked up the courage to tell my husband exactly what I thought of his baby idea. That babies shouldn't be marriage-fixers, that I was too old, we were too busy and he was never around. All perfectly solid reasons, right?

But the next morning my mouth had decided for me that, at the end of the day, Julian *should* experience the joys (the pains were all for moms) of fatherhood. And that he was definitely worth nine months of gastric reflux, chronic backache and swollen feet. (He liked me even when I was cranky.) So I told him.

"We should do it," I said while we were lounging around, the kids still in bed.

"Do what?" he asked, looking up from his paper.

"You know, the kid thing," I whispered into my mug, feeling my face go hot.

Rustling of paper. Intake of breath. His. I was already holding mine.

"Really, Erica?" he whispered.

I put my mug down and straightened my hair, flashing him my version of the famous Cantelli smile- all teeth and no confidence whatsoever. Because

Renata's words kept ringing in my ears. *A baby makes a marriage.* Did I really agree with her? My mind said I didn't. My heart told me I was crazy, but *me* was terrified of getting pregnant for all the wrong reasons. All I could think was *What if we do need a baby to change things?*

"Yeah, absolutely. I've thought about it. I'm ready."

Julian squeezed my hand and dropped a delicious kiss on my lips.

Judy and Renata, zero- my marriage, one.

*

"Keep your legs up, sweetheart," Julian whispered as he finally pulled out of me later that evening. Did I say *finally*? I didn't mean it like that, but he was really taking his time. I mean, don't get me wrong- he has never been hasty in the bedroom- on the contrary, Julian's always been deliciously thorough- but now, it was like he wanted to make extra-sure his parcel had been delivered and signed for. I sure hoped it would work. I hated to see Julian disappointed.

But then again, not being a parent would actually spare him some major disappointments. Like when your kids become teenagers and eat the flower of Superior Knowledge? Suddenly they know everything and all *you* are is a blooming idiot.

Nothing you say holds its weight anymore, you've lost all your clout and they spend more time in their bedroom doing God knows what (we only had a telephone and magazines, plus the occasional joint- what harm could we get up to?).

But this generation- if you so much as even *looked* at them in a manner they didn't like you'd get a shower of expletives that would last you a week.

But a mother's gotta be a mother, no matter what. I was the opposite of my own flaky, glamorous stand-in mom in every way. Besides, I used to be a hotel manager where everybody snapped to the sound of my voice. And to be honest, I liked exercising my authority over my children while I still could. And boy did I make sure I did it thoroughly. It wouldn't be long before my own two were transformed into the monsters I've heard so much about.

"No, Maddy. You can't wear high heels. They're bad for your back and Mila is against them. And I'm against them."

"Mo-om!"

"They ruin your posture. Besides, you're already five foot eight."

"Mila knows nothing," she huffed. "She says I'm no good at ballet because I'm too tall. She says it, like, slows me down or something."

I took a long hard look at my daughter. Mila had a point. Her long legs gave her a funny gait that her hips hadn't quite yet mastered. While Angelica had already filled out, Maddy was still on the slender side and, I suspect, a little jealous of her friend's confidence. As much as Maddy flaunted her prettiness at home and acted cool in front of her friends, I knew she was scared of not being accepted. She was the terrified leader who was waiting to be caught out for not believing in herself. Remind you of anyone?

But there was a big difference between us. Maddy was afraid of *others* not appreciating her. She personally appreciated herself immensely, and when she referred to her thighs as ham joints, she didn't really mean it. Apparently it was the thing to talk bad about your body nowadays. Today when girls say they don't like their body they mean they absolutely love it. In my days, when we didn't love our bodies we just shut the hell up and hoped to go through life unnoticed.

So if her dreams of ballet dancing were quickly disappearing, was she really aiming towards being a model as she had lately announced? Please God, no. She had artistic talent and a flair for fashion. Why not put it to work as a fashion designer? But ultimately whatever she decided to be, I only hoped the definition included the word *happy*.

Which made me wonder if I had been an adequate mother after all my efforts. And while asking myself what kind of a mother I was, I wondered what I had got myself into by agreeing to have another kid. Blimey, as

Julian would say, did I really have any clue? Kids these days were more difficult to handle- they weren't the shy, docile idiots we- well, *I* was once upon a life ago. These kids today were like tsunamis. If you didn't want to get in their path you had to run to higher grounds and pray for damage control. Which I did.

"Madeleine," I finally concluded. "I'm not discussing high-heeled shoes any further with you. Now go wash your hands and set the table." Maybe I was still in time to retract my promise to Julian?

*

Ironically, a few weeks later I found out Julian's precious parcel had actually *arrived*.

I stared at the stick, my mouth opening and closing like a fish's. A pregnant fish. Pregnant. I was actually, *really*, pregnant. At my age, what were the odds the minute I went off birth-control? Had Julian speed-delivery *ordered* the kid?

To be honest, I can't say I was overjoyed. I could have been happy, but joy was overclouded by The Big Doubt- why Julian wanted this baby in the first place. He had a career, a business, two step-children whom although he loved very much, had given him much ado the past eight years. Why go through it all over again just when you think it's finally over?

"Exactly why do you want to be a father, again?" I asked Julian as we were finishing dinner that night, this big piece of news burning a hole up my sleeve.

Julian pushed his now empty plate forward and folded the tablecloth over to rest his arms on the clean, crumb-less underside. Although I hated it when he did that, tonight I hardly noticed.

"Erica... are you having second thoughts?"

"Of course not. I'm... happy to do this. And..." I flashed him a shy grin, "...that's one thing we can cross off our list now by the way."

"What?"

I smiled, pushing the crumbs before me into one little pile. "Baby Mission accomplished, baby..."

His eyes widened. "What? You're... *pregnant?*"

The look on his face told me that there was no crisis to worry about. Sod Renata, Judy and their paranoia. This man was in love with me, no doubt.

I smiled. "Uh-huh..."

"I'm going to be a father!" Julian yelled, lifting me and twirling me around the kitchen like in a cheesy Monday afternoon movie. But the look in his eyes opened up a new world to me. A world I never knew existed. Jesus- all these years he'd wanted to be a father and never *told* me? What did that say about our marriage? Paradoxically, now I was even more worried than before.

"Oh, sweetheart, that's so surreal!" he chimed, kissing my lips, his green eyes bright. "We'll decorate the study and paint-"

"The study? But you *love* your study!" I argued. "That's your sacred ground! You don't let anyone in there."

"But a baby's a baby! Honey, we're going to be parents!"

I already was one, and so was he, but pointing that out would be party-pooping at this point. Still I had to draw the line somewhere. "Hold your horses, Julian. I haven't even had an official blood test yet."

"You don't need one. I *know* you're pregnant."

Yes, so did I.

*

Surreal, Julian had called my pregnancy. It turned out he was right. It was a surreal, three-week pregnancy. Then a major, major period. And according to my doctor, Dottoressa Bardotti, probably one of my last.

The thought was unbearable and I swallowed and nodded in a business-like manner as she sat us down with my file and test results. When I explained our situation she blinked. I tried to convince myself it was just a reflex or a spasm, but who was I kidding?

"Hmmm…" she said, flipping through my file, and by the time she looked up I was hanging on the edge of my seat as Julian squeezed my hand under the table, paler than my grandmother's linen embroidered sheets.

"So you're looking to get pregnant," she said matter-of-factly and I almost expected her to add, like Judy, *What the hell for?* "Well, given your age I suggest we get a move on. Every month is precious, you understand."

No, I didn't understand. I had always been *very* fertile. Hadn't it been for birth control I'd have stocked the NFL team given enough time.

And now this woman was telling me I was a monthly time-bomb, waiting to go off, that is, to dry up into arid, horrid menopause? She was practically saying that if we didn't crack our eggs pronto there would *be* no baby. Great. Why did Julian decide *now* that he wanted a child? Why hadn't he told me before, preferably eight years ago when I was still bursting with eggs like a bloody Mexican piñata?

I had been happy with Julian and the kids. But now, as you can imagine, hearing the doctor say that I couldn't do it was more than a challenge to me. I had failure-phobia, not because I had never failed, but because I had failed only too many times. Hearing Dottoressa Bardotti say that becoming parents wouldn't exactly be a cinch because we only had a margin of virtually what- twelve, twenty-four more periods if I was lucky- triggered in me a number of contrasting, gut-wrenching feelings.

She explained that as I'd had my period very young I would very probably face menopause earlier than most women.

So there you go- once again, fat had managed, even retroactively, to ruin my life. There was no escaping from it. My weight had kept me a social pariah throughout my school years. It kept me standing against the wall at my high school prom (Peter DeVita was long gone by then, and Tony Esposito had dropped out, thank God.)

I thought I could beat the effects of fat on my life with a good job, but even then fat had left me sweating buckets on my first job interviews, making me look like a real loser. Fat did nothing good.

But I'll always be grateful to Mr. Farthington who didn't care about looks and just wanted the job done. He got me as far as I wanted. But life was not full of Mr. Farthingtons. Life was teaming with young, skinny-assed women having children right, left and center.

Sometimes I wished I could be a thin, non-existent paper doll, like one of Maddy's childhood, pretty-in-pink, lifeless creations. You know, all legs and no heart to break, no soul to ache. Paul (my BGFF who travelled between the US and Italy for work), Maddy and I would sit for hours on end at our kitchen table back in Boston and draw all sorts of outfits for these size zero sticks. Everything looked good on them. Funny how no one's ever made a pregnant paper doll. I imagined drawing one with an eight-month bulge, but in

2-D she'd only look *fat*. And would have to wear dark droopy clothes.

And to think I'd got over all this. To think I had finally reached a stage where I was ok with everything. My weight was still too much. Countless doctors had told me I was never going to be a stick figure, so eight years ago, at seventy-five kilos and thirty-five years of age I had come to terms with myself and had started to accept myself- and more desserts as well.

Now I had gained ten kilos worth of apple pies, gelato and *biscotti*. I'd *tried* dieting but my weight yo-yoed miserably. Even when I temporarily got back to seventy-five kilograms, I was always told that The Former Me had the upper hand. Because my lifestyle as a fat woman had taken charge of me, ruining me for good.

And if at first having Julian's baby wasn't exactly on my Top Five Things To Do Before You Die, now it had become a *necessity*. Not just because I'd wanted to make Julian happy, but also because I needed to succeed in this relationship. My previous marriage had left me devastated. I couldn't be a loser any more. I had lost most of the battles in my life and was just beginning to savor an equilibrium with myself. The kids were doing great. Julian was doing great. Me, I wasn't so sure anymore.

But when I thought about it (because now I could hardly think of anything else), I actually *missed* the nausea, the all-nighters, the endless, sleepless nights of dragging myself out of bed. Was I nuts or what?

*

My doctor gave us a list of tests to run, first of all- you guessed it- Julian's sperm. It turned out to be super-sperm (why was I not surprised?), particularly lively and healthy. I could almost imagine them not swimming but *shooting* around in the Petri dish, showing off. *Look at me! Wee! I can zing and dart across the universe if I want to! Yay! I'm Supersperm!* And all that while my little, *old* eggs watched in awe, thinking, "Oh, he'll never want to stick around *us*!"

Well, at least we now knew it was all my fault. And so the ordeal began. By ordeal I mean a one-thousand-two-hundred-calorie-per-day diet to up my chances of conceiving because, as per Dottoressa Bardotti, there was no point in IVF or anything of the sort if I weighed what I weighed. Prior to the procedure I'd have to take fertility drugs that would have the same effect on me as on a cow, (yes, she really said that) i.e, none whatsoever, unless I lost weight. *Lots of it.*

But because time was running out, I took hormones against my doctor's *professional* advice, although, between you and me, she said, "What the heck, go for it- it's now or never." I guess female solidarity stretched beyond professional boundaries. Fine by me.

So if on one side I was supposed to be losing weight, on the other side they were fattening me up with artificial crap intended to make me more fertile but in actuality was only making me more bloated. And turning me into a raging bitch. No one could say anything to me that didn't sound like a compliment. Even the slam of a door would ignite me and I'd burst into tears.

"Sweetheart," Julian said to me the first third time it happened. "I don't want you in this state. Let's not do this."

To his credit, he was concerned for me. But after weeks of munching on carrots and rice cakes, I had passed the point of no return. Reverting to my previous eating habits would've been bliss, but I didn't want to blow the whole thing off and dash Julian's hopes. He'd done so much for me in the past eight years.

Now I wanted to do this for him. He deserved it. But, truth be said, my motherly instincts weren't getting much satisfaction these days with my own two. Warren was always in Siena at university and the less Maddy saw me nowadays the better it was.

CHAPTER SIX: Hysterosalpingography Hysteria

To be on the safe side, and because I couldn't believe it was only my fat ass stopping us from having a baby when all around me enormous women my age were getting pregnant, I had some routine tests done to make sure all my hardware was in place.

The first, a Hysterosalpingography, was to determine whether my tubes were clogged or not via sticking a catheter way up there with a dye that spread all around and into them. If the dye reached the end of my tubes unhindered, it meant they weren't blocked and we were home free.

They wouldn't let Julian in with me because of the X-rays so I lay sprawled on a table with my feet up in the stirrups while a guy I'd never met before (I know I'm a bit old fashioned but at least a *Hello* would have sufficed) told me it wasn't going to hurt in the least and shoved this contraption way up inside me.

"Yeowhh!" I hollered, seeing spots, and they all stood above me bewildered while I was doing my best not to pass out from the pain as he ripped my insides apart.

"Impossibile," another guy said shoving (that is the only word that comes to mind, believe me) the

instrument even further up. "It shouldn't hurt, this is not normal."

"How come no one ever told you your uterus is *retroflesso*?" the doctor barked at me.

"Retro*what*?"

"What's the word? Abnormal? No, tipped."

Believe me, if I hadn't had that thing inside me, I'd have jumped off the table and headed for the hills. Abnormal, my uterus? It had worked just fine for the last forty-three years.

"Oh, no, no it's okay- false alarm. It's just the speculum that's broken inside her," he said to no one in particular. "Can I get a new one, somebody, please?"

And this was a private, expensive fertility clinic. I wondered what would've happened if I had been poor and sent to just any doctor. But then I realized that if I had been too poor to afford a fertility clinic the babies would have spilled out of me like in Shrek's nightmare. I refused to let my mind wander that far.

And so, the doctors looking down on me, all smiles, we waited for an unbroken speculum to arrive from the bowels of the clinic.

"Live nearby?" one doctor actually asked me. I raised my evil eyebrow at him and he got the message and turned away.

On the way back to the doctor's office on the ground floor, the walls began to move and my vision blur.

"I don't feel so good," I managed before everything went black.

When I came to, I was overwhelmed with the urge to hurl, so I tried to sit up from a gurney they must've put me on, but the doctor kept pushing me onto my back.

Damn you, you want me to choke on my own vomit- let me sit up! I wanted to scream, my face cold and clammy, my lips shaking, but when I gagged he finally understood and helped me up. So much for an understanding and empathic vocation.

Julian was holding my hand, his face pale.

"I'm okay now," I wheezed, trying to fill my lungs and get up, but both Julian ad the doctor pushed me back down again, Julian tearing off a piece of paper towel from a roll behind him and wiping my forehead.

"Your blood pressure just plummeted," the doctor explained, his fingers tight around my wrist, checking my heartbeat.

So did my faith in you, you butcher, shot through my mind, but luckily all that made it to my mouth was "I'm okay now." I whispered to Julian, "I want to get up now. Please."

But both men shook their heads.

"You're not going anywhere until I'm sure you're okay," Julian said.

The doctor said nothing, his hand on my wrist, eyes on his watch.

My heart was beating like a drum, but mostly, I don't know why, I felt... humiliated. Like an animal in a slaughterhouse. I had never come this close to my physical fragility before. All my life I'd fought like a tigress to be like other people by using my mind, while my body had simply been something my mind dragged along behind it. And the fact that my body was now in the limelight, what with the IVF and tests, only made me feel inadequate by tenfold.

So being all bruised up on the inside, I did the only thing I could do- keep it light.

"I must've given him a scare and a half in there," I forced a grin as Julian and I were finally driving home an hour later. "There was enough material in there today for a lawsuit."

"Never mind him- you scared the crap out of *me*," Julian said. "What am I going to do without you if you drop down dead?"

"Be free," I quipped and he cast me a stern look which melted immediately the moment our eyes met. Yeah, he'd take it really nastily if I croaked, of that I was sure. Good man.

"Seriously, Erica- why are we doing this? I can only imagine what happened to you in there to make you feel like that. You're no queasy girl."

That was true.

"So... what exactly did happen... in there?"

I told him, the speculum thing snapping included and I went all clammy again. He went white himself and squeezed my hand.

"Forget it, sweetheart. I don't want you doing this. It's not worth it."

"Oh, but it is," I assured him. "It's like no other feeling in the world, Julian. I don't want you to miss out on that."

As he slowed down to yield to a tractor at the intersection near our home, he turned to look at me, his eyes soft. I really didn't want him to miss out on the joy of cradling your own kid- something that is incommensurable. There is nothing like that in this world. And I'd do anything to give Julian that now.

I caressed the back of his hand. "I'll be fine, Julian. I'm a tough girl."

If anything, I knew I needed to become tougher. My current amount of tough wasn't going to cut it.

In the following days Julian and I read up on fertility treatments and, just for fun, some fertility myths so out of this world they made you wonder whether there actually was some truth to them, like sex on a daily basis (which Julian strongly advocated), headstands, and others that only a man could have made up.

"Get this," Julian read as I nestled into the crook of his arm. "The consumption of yams, grapefruit juice and even stinging nettles find a scientific justification as far as an increase in fertility may be concerned."

I sat up. "I have to swallow stinging nettles too?"

He chuckled. "Silly." Then: "Would you?"

"Anything for you, Julian."

He put his laptop down and stared at me. The silence was deafening.

"What?" I said.

"I love you, Erica."

I climbed up his body. "Enough to drive into town for a delicious *Torta Cecina*?"

He laughed. "You already having cravings?"

I shrugged. "Might as well start practising."

So yes, I was on a diet but rewarded myself once in a while for my efforts. It wasn't like I was doing pushups and knocking down Ferrero Rocher chocolates (another weakness of mine) lined up on the terracotta tiles on the down-stroke.

Soon we'd be ready for IVF. But that didn't stop us from researching every single fertility myth, including religious candles and prayer- anything that looked like someone had pulled them out of the pages of a medieval sorcerer's How To Cast A Spell book.

And neither in the bedroom, I soon discovered, did Julian want to take any chances. So he continued taking his time. I waited as he got his breathing back to normal, his head hanging low between his shoulders until he sank on top of me and went still, my leg still bent back against my chest as if I was doing bench presses, and in a way, I was. You try keeping a six-foot-three, two hundred and twenty pound man off you with the sole strength of your thigh muscles.

Many minutes had passed. How long did he actually think I could stay pretzeled like that? Had he passed out? He sure was overworking himself in between the sheets lately. Had he had a stroke and died, or was he simply sleeping? Now *that* would have been a real boost to my ego.

While I was mulling these possibilities over, a sharp pain shot through my leg. "Ow, ow, ow, *cramp*!" I screeched, letting my leg fall back down and knocking Julian over the head, but it seemed to reactivate him. "Oh, I'm so sorry!" I cried.

"Don't worry," he whispered. "Are you okay?"

Okay? He'd really fallen asleep on me. But I couldn't blame the guy- I was exhausted myself while only doing the minimal amount of work.

"I'm fine." I tried not to sound snappy. "I'm not the one that got knocked over the head."

"No sweat, I've got a hard head."

Apparently not only that. I stared at him and then looked down. "Are you... *already*?"

"Ready for another round? Absolutely."

"But I'm not..."

"That's okay, have a nap."

A nap? I wanted to sleep for a week! We'd been doing this all week around my 'fertile window' and I was exhausted. I had forgotten Julian had all that stamina. I'd forgotten *I'd* had all that strength in the past. But, I was determined- hell-bent for this to work. So onward and upward towards ultimate joy.

*

And so came the day of our first IVF cycle. I'll spare you the fear, the hope, but most of all the look on Julian's face when they handed him a plastic container. What did he think his part was, just holding my hand and cheering me on with a *'Push!'* at the very end?

I gave him the thumbs up and a "Go for it" as he dismally disappeared into the next room.

Just to spare you the wait, the first cycle didn't take. So over the months began the long string of attempts and it turned out Julian was having more encounters with that plastic container than with me. Not that we didn't want to have sex anymore- far from it- but we were both exhausted from the stress of it all, and on the weekends the kids were home most of the time so instead of losing ourselves in the luxury of lust on the kitchen table and every other stick of furniture in the house as we used to, we would fall asleep in each other's arms as soon as our backs hit the bed.

But even at the end of another good day, our 'us time' over a cappuccino on the veranda while soaking up yet another spectacular sunset, there was always that big fat question, hanging between us like an enormous piñata that wanted to be flogged to death: Why couldn't I *naturally* give the love of my life what he wanted most- a child of his own blood? And, more to the point, would there be a shift in our relationship if I couldn't, pun intended, *deliver*?

And to make things worse, everywhere I looked, suddenly almost every woman was pregnant. From the butcher's wife to Maddy's dance teacher (the one that was so harsh on Maddy but flirted shamelessly with Julian) and nearly every woman in the supermarket. It was as if an epidemic had broken out in the entire province of Siena and I'd been immune.

And you should have seen some of these pregnant women. The ones that got to me the most were the young, tall, slim fashionable girls with great jobs in the city that were as gorgeous as ever, not encumbered by the extra weight but effortlessly sporting the cutest little bumps. One woman, whom I had dubbed Sporty Spice because of her pigtails and gym suits, had a collection of T-shirts she wore to the market with a decal of a beach-ball on it.

No- I lied. What hurt me more was seeing the *historically huge* women pregnant. I mean, we're talking one hundred and over kilograms. If fat was a fertility inhibitor, how the hell did *they* manage to get knocked up? Every time I got my period it was a freaking tragedy lately. For weeks I'd be thinking, *this time it'll work, this time I'll get pregnant. We did it at the right time, I can feel it.* But it never happened. My period seemed very proud to be smack on time, thwarting our every hope.

I hadn't even been thinking about having a baby until I was told I couldn't. And now all I could think about was a girl with Julian's eyes or a boy with his calm disposition. I could already see them, just an egg-meets-sperm away. No biggie. It was the most natural thing in the world. People all over the world had sex and got pregnant. Any day now…

CHAPTER SEVEN: The Home-wrecker Calleth

The next week while Julian was away I was juggling my laundry bin, holding it against my hip as I struggled to get the back door open, the portable phone jammed between my cheek and shoulder. It was Terry Peterson, Julian's New York agent.

"Erica? I got cut off from Julian's cell. Just tell him that they loved the book. The Brazilian butt got lots of laughs."

Brazilian butt?
"Uh, okay, thanks, Terry. I'll tell him."

I ventured into Julian's office that was off-limits because he was very secretive about his work. Everywhere there were file folders with fact sheets and on his cork-board, cut-outs of homes, cars, people and even pets, believe it or not. I thought only romance novelists did that, you know, to re-create a fictitious world. My Julian was so *cute*.

All I knew so far was that his hero was a baseball player who couldn't get a contract and ended up drinking and gambling his life away. That, to my knowledge, was not autobiographical. Feeling a bit guilty but too curious to stop myself, I turned on his laptop opened the document containing his novel. Then I immediately clicked on *Find* and typed in "Brazilian".

It was just a little, innocent peek. A peek that would suffice me for the rest of my life. I caught a glimpse of the words, *'and a butt like a Brazilian carnival dancer'*. Brazilian butt? *Brazilian butt?* I leaned forward against his desk, my eyes skimming furtively for more. Okay, so he liked Brazilian butts. What man didn't? But how come I'd never heard him say anything similar before? It was obvious. Because I didn't have a Brazilian butt and never *would*.

And all these years he'd seen my butt and thought, *I wish she had a Brazilian butt.* Ouch. That really woke me up. Good thing I'd started dieting again. Only it made me really really cranky. Maybe I could take up Pilates seriously and get some massages at the local beautician to shed a few pounds a bit quicker? The last time I'd seen her was to get my legs waxed the previous summer. Ok, so maybe I needed to get down there more often.

Stop it, I scolded myself. *You're getting all worked up because of two words in a one-hundred k* (that's what the header said) *novel.* Really, how insecure can a woman be? He loved me, and what was most important, *I* loved me. Most of the time. So enough. I had dinner to make. But as it was, I scrolled up and started to read, feeling my face go hot.

The heroine was a beautiful blonde celebrity, all boobs and legs. Her name was Chastity (no surname) and she was a game-show host's assistant and always walked onto the stage with little more than a bright smile and prizes for the contestants. She was the object of the hero's sleepless nights, and the male audience was in rapture every time she turned to leave because she had a butt like- to the point- a Brazilian Carnival dancer.

*

As promised, Julian was back in record time for our Spider Anniversary, i.e., the day we'd first met and he'd ripped my clothes off straight away. (How's that for a promising start?)

I'd had the evening of our lives planned out for him, which had three basic ingredients. Julian, me and a ton of whip cream. (And, well, yes, okay, chocolate cake, too).

Remember when once upon a time I said only a bomb on our house could shake Julian? That bomb arrived precisely the day before our seventh wedding anniversary after I got back from my beautician's.

The amount of things I'd had done there was longer than a grocery list- leg wax , armpits, bikini line), face peeling, face massage, eyebrow tweezing, a manicure, a pedicure and almost a brain lobotomy. Suffice to say I spent at least three hours in there.

Then off to the hairdresser's and finally to Siena to buy him a gift, even though I always ended up getting him the usual Polo shirt or riding boots.

So, with my face still kind of swollen from the waxing and plucking, I kept a low profile, trying to stay away from Julian's sight, but the bugger always insisted on helping me clean up after dinner. He said he didn't feel right sitting in the snug with his feet up if I wasn't relaxing too. That's one of the reasons I didn't marry an Italian.

Anyway, I was washing and Julian was drying when the phone went. He stretched out a damp hand and held the earpiece between his cheek and shoulder, said "A Taste of Tuscany, *Buonasera*," and listened as I turned the tap off.

"Speaking," he answered, eyes narrowing.

I stopped and watched as his eyebrows shot up. "Genie Stacie? I can't believe it! How *are* you?"

The voice, which I could hear as clearly as a bell, was high-pitched and babbling. She went on and on and Julian glanced at me, guiltily (at least that's what I think now) and nodded, repetitively, trying to get a word in edge-wise.

"Yes, but how- sure, but- when would you-?"

In the end he hung up, dazed.

"Who the *hell* was that?" I chuckled.

He scratched his head. "An old friend of mine, Genie Stacie. We dated for a spell ages ago. She found me through my agent. She's in the area, so…"

"Genie Stacie? As in the model slash actress Genie Stacie?"

"Uh, yes…"

Julian had dated *her*? She was possibly the prettiest thing in Hollywood, with long long legs, a slender frame and a mane of platinum blonde hair. She'd been on the cover of Sports Illustrated more times than I could count. She'd had a whirlwind romance with Scottish actor Tom Jackson a few years ago and had had a kid as a result. I knew all this because she was also, God help us, Maddy's idol. It was thanks to Genie Stacie's lack of taste and dignity that I'd had to speak to my daughter about her haste to grow up and the length of her skirts.

"She says she needs to come and see me," Julian informed me, his gaze lost in an imaginary maze of memories.

"Needs?"

Julian shrugged, his hand stealing to the back of his neck, rubbing softly. Funny- in eight years I'd never ever seen him do that before. It was like a sign of… embarrassment.

"She said she's in a bit of trouble, and that only I can help her."

"Hmm… I wonder what kind of trouble?"

"I'm not quite sure. She didn't elaborate. I said it's okay. Is it okay?" he asked dubiously.

You invite a sex-bomb into our home where we have a twenty-year-old boy who's chomping at the bit to be a man and a sixteen-year-old-girl who thinks she is Genie Stacie and ask me if it's okay?

"Sure," I said, sporting a smile I didn't feel. Please God, not that pre-divorce, teeth-baring grin again. I couldn't stand it. It had taken me eight years to gain a modicum of self-confidence, and now this. I got a terrible feeling. I was also getting a terrible migraine.

"She'll be here tomorrow afternoon around six," Julian informed me.

"On our anniversary and just in time for dinner," I said, not bothering to hide the sarcasm in my voice.

"I was going to take you to *L'Archetto*," Julian said as he took my hand and kissed it.

Damn, my favorite restaurant. I sighed. "Forget it. What should I cook? What does she eat?"

Julian thought about it. "Nothing, if I remember correctly. Genie Stacie eats practically nothing."

It figured. I turned the tap on, and an awkward silence fell as we finished our evening chores.

"I'll make it up to you, I promise," he whispered, nuzzling my neck.

"Damn right you will," I assured him. Then I turned off the water again, a terrible thought mushrooming in my mind. "Are you going to fall in love with her all over again and dump me?" I said and stopped, unable to believe I'd actually said it.

He looked up at me, surprised, not sure whether I was joking or not. I put on my
'I'm just kidding' face and rolled my eyes, but he still watched me. Damn, he knew me better than I thought.

"First of all, honey, I was never in love with her. Not really," he said, leaning in to kiss me on the lips. What the heck did that mean? How can you *not really* love someone? Either you do or you don't.

"Now let's go upstairs. Unless you want me to take you on the kitchen floor?"

I batted my lashes like they do in the movies. "Maddy and Warren'll be gone for hours."

"Hours it is, then," said my tantric husband with a grin as he took the dishcloth from my shoulder and pulled me upstairs. Not that I was resisting, mind you. And by midnight we were cuddling, just about to doze off, when Julian whispered to me, "Happy Seventh Anniversary, Mrs. Foxham."

CHAPTER EIGHT: The Home-wrecker Cometh

So... Genie Stacie Grant. Model slash actress, typical blonde bombshell all legs and no brain. I looked closer at her butt in the magazine ads. As much as it was perfect, it didn't *quite* have that Brazilian edge I'd imagined. Maybe because of the lack of a tan. But then I flipped the page there she was again, only this time her skin was the color of leather, and sand had been strewn down her back, almost a continuation of her long blonde hair that reached her waist, and a bikini thong was shoved between her butt cheeks. Now those *looked* very Brazilian.

All this time. All this time Julian had known her, had cherished the memories of sex with her lithe, lean form while my ripples of fat threatened to bury him like a tsunami wave.

*

"Genie Stacie? Here in our house? Oh my *God*!" Maddy squealed, jumping up and down. Susie looked up at her and yapped, happy to see Maddy excited about something for a change. "I have to get my hair done! I need a new dress and-"

"Hold your horses there, Missy," I cautioned as I dished up lunch. Four hours to Genie Stacie's arrival and I was already a wreck. But hopefully- and there was the trick- *nowhere* near showing it.

"And Maddy- remember to act your age. She's not your best friend." *Or mine*, I added mentally.

"But Mo-om! Genie Stacie is *the* sex icon! She is like, the *it* girl! She is sooo-"

Didn't I know it. After Julian had fallen asleep the night before, I did what any balanced, self-assured woman would do- I Googled her. And boy was I sorry. For a couple that had only dated briefly there were way too many pictures of them together. Parties, award ceremonies, luncheons, dinners, holidays abroad- the works.

And he was all over her; his arm around her non-existent waist, his face in a constant smile. The same smile that had kept me sane all these years. The smile I'd thought was just for me. How naïve could I have been?

And then there were just as many photos of her on her own or with the other rogues she'd dated. She was always in the tabloids for her party-going and her men.

Tom Jackson had been half decent but even that hadn't lasted. And now this man-eater was coming to our home, back into Julian's life. A shiver ran up my arms and over my neck, making the little hairs on my skin stand. Whatever it was she needed to see him for, it would not be good.

Sure, very often we had writers, actors and actresses staying with us when they wanted total privacy, but this one shared a history with my husband.

Of all our returning guests, my absolute favorite was romance writer Elizabeth Jennings. She came to stay at A Taste of Tuscany at least once a year and always kept in touch.

Originally from a small town in Oregon, she moved to Florence when she was a teenager. Love had sent her to southern Italy where she literally carved out of the rocks what is known today as the Women's Fiction Festival- an event you have to see to believe.

Writers, publishers, agents and all kinds of media experts from around the world meet in Matera every September to join in the feast of writing, eating, drinking and talking shop. Of course I'm not a writer- I just go for the food and the amazing company of brilliant people who love what they do.

But it hadn't always been like that for Elizabeth. Years and years spent travelling and living out of her suitcase as an interpreter and making enormous sacrifices, she was now finally where she wanted to be, free to write from her heart and enjoying every word of it.

If anyone knew Julian- or any other Alpha male- it was Elizabeth. She had written the book- well, actually, *the books* on men like him, outrageously masculine, protective and dedicated to the well-being of their woman no matter the cost.

Her Alpha male principal pretty much applied to Julian- in his earlier days. Years ago Julian would have fought for me like Elizabeth's men fight for their women, like when he'd knocked down my front door to save the kids and me from Ira's baseball bat. But nowadays I wasn't so sure.

Elizabeth hadn't been here an hour and I'd already told her about my insecurities where Julian was concerned and she sipped her wine, her eyes never leaving my face. I could see the wheels turning and knew she'd deliver me the rock-solid, elementary facts as usual.

"Sweetie, Julian is still living here with you."

"Well, yes, of course, but-"

"Then that says it all. He's never been the type of guy to stay in a relationship that didn't fit him."

I thought about it and realized she was right. If he lived here with me it was because he wanted to. Why couldn't I reach the same conclusions on my own?

"Men like him don't come along so often in life, you know that," she said, giving me a little nudge. "Think of all you've been through and how he was always there for you. What else do you want from the poor guy?"

I looked up at her. Elizabeth was confident, successful, talented. And above all she always had it together. I could learn so much from her- and not just about relationships. "You're so right!"

She grinned. "I know! The two of you need to get away from your getaway. Come to Matera for a while. Visit the *Sassi*. Stay at the Spa."

Which got me thinking of all the good food I'd had there and I was hungry all over again. "Hey, let's go to *L'Archetto* restaurant," I suggested. "They have these amazing *antipasti* that make your mouth water from the other side of the dining hall. We'll drink, eat, talk and you can give me a sneak preview of what you're working on."

She smiled. "Now you're talking sense, girl."

*

"Mom, do I look okay? Can I wear make-up just this once?"

Just this once? Who did she think she was fooling? I saw the traces of foundation on her clothes and saw the make-up remover in her bathroom. But today I was picking my battles very carefully in view of the biblical one I had coming against Genie Stacie.

"I don't think so, Maddy. Hurry up and get your ballet stuff. When you get back you'll meet her."

She frowned. "Can't I just skip ballet lessons this afternoon, Mom, please? Just this once?"

"Skip ballet lessons? You're always telling me how you get massacred when you miss a single one or if you're even two minutes late."

"Yeah, I know, but I'll make it up to Mila."

"No, you won't."

"Let her, Mom," Warren said as he came in, kicking off his dusty shoes at the door. "Otherwise it'll be hell until then."

I turned and snorted. "The only hell that we're going to have here is if you people start losing your heads because a peroxide, paper doll walks into our home." Didn't I sound just a teensy bit jealous? Tough bananas. I was the mother and had to set the example of moral discipline.

"Mom, you have to adapt to the times," Warren insisted.

"The hell I do. Especially if it means allowing my daughter to act like I've taught her absolutely nothing," I said, opening the fridge and taking a swig of milk directly from the bottle, just like I always forbade them to.

"Hey, what are my two favorite girls in the world doing?" Julian called as he appeared in the doorway behind Warren, toeing his own sneakers off. He stopped when he saw me drinking and wiping my mouth with the back of my hand.

"Bad morning?" he asked.

"Dad! Mom won't let me see Genie Stacie today!"

I sighed. "That's not true. I just don't want her to skip her ballet class."

"That sounds like good advice to me," he agreed as Warren plunked himself down, all sweaty and grinning, on a chair and chugged down a bottle of apple juice. I glared at him to remind him of his manners and he nodded at the bottle of milk in my hands.

"Just think- Stefania's gonna kill me when she finds out!" Warren whistled.
"And that makes you happy?" I asked.
"Absolutely! It pushes my stock up!"
"Oh, get over yourself, you pig," Maddy hissed. "You think someone like supermodel Genie Stacie is even going to look at a slob like you?"

"I'm not a slob," he said, burping. "Sorry."

Julian grinned at me, then turned to Maddy. "Language, my little lady," he whispered and Maddy turned pink. "Sorry, Dad. It's just that Mom drives me crazy."

"Likewise," I said, pushing the boys out. Go wash up, you two. We don't want a diva to see the real us." Although I knew she'd seen the real Julian- all six foot three inches of him.

I opened the car door and Maddy plunked herself next to me in a huff and we took off down our squiggly

97

private road that led to Castellino, my mind still on bloody Genie Stacie.

Just when I thought I'd managed to be what I wanted to be. A mother and a housewife that had time to cook and didn't have to worry about wearing a suit to work. And just when I had started to get comfortable, I was expected to compare with bloody Genie Stacie.

The hours dragged by. Deciding what to wear hadn't been a problem for me in the last eight years. It was pretty simple- sundresses and flip flops when it was warm, jeans when it was cold. Oh, and track suits around the house, for when I'm cleaning or cooking (which is practically always). So what could I wear now in the presence of The It Girl, my daughter's teen idol and my husband's former lover that wouldn't melt me right into the background?

I thumbed through my unutilized wardrobe, having thrown all my old American stuff away- business suits and post-diet outfits, but still considered as Plus Sizes Made In Italy.

My beautiful green Krizia jersey dress looked like my best option, but it was too pretty, making me look like I was trying too hard. How about my black dress? For God's sake, could I do any worse? It had *I don't know what else to wear* all over it, like I had no imagination. Truth be told, all the imagination on earth wouldn't find me the right dress. Because there was *nothing* I could wear that wouldn't make me look like a complete nobody next to her. A *fat* nobody. I sighed. Here we go again. In one afternoon I'd morphed from a happy-ish, satisfied and confident woman into an insecure teenager. Thanks to a model I hardly knew existed, like all those dolls inhabiting fashion magazines.

Jeans? Jeans said *I don't give a hoot, this is what I'd have worn anyway because your presence doesn't threaten me in the least. So there.*

At a quarter to six, I put on a brave smile, or at least I tried to, but I ended up baring my teeth like I used to in my pre-Julian, pre-Tuscany days. Years of killing my demons, and now they were back- in the flesh of Genie Stacie. Luckily, in a few hours' time this would be over and Genie Stacie out of our lives.

*

Of course she arrived in a sports car wearing a pink-colored mini-dress that looked like a baby doll nightie. She wore no bra and I suspect not even any panties, so seamless was her perfect butt. I noticed because she had her back to me as she threw herself at Julian, the skimpy dress riding high up her thighs, her inexistent belly against his. Boy, she was a tall thing. Even taller than me.

"Oh, my God, Julian," I missed you *soooo muuuch!*" she cried, her shrill voice piercing my eardrums from where I was standing, I couldn't imagine what it did to Julian's at that distance. But he smiled and released himself from her grip, holding his arm out to me.

She looked just like the blonde in Julian's novel, or at least the image I'd formed in my mind. *Bloody hell.* The taut, Brazilian butt. This was Chastity's reincarnation. The image that Julian had worked around, all this time.

"Genie Stacie, this is Erica."

"Oh, Julian, it's so typical of you to hire local help! Does she speak English?"

Julian glanced at me. "Uh, actually, Erica is my wife."

She turned to look at me. "Right, very funny, Julian, very funny."

After I'd assembled something next to a fake smile and said, "Pleased to meet you, Genie Stacie. Welcome to our home." Thirty seconds and she had already managed to piss me off royally.

She put her hand to her mouth and said, "Oh, I'm so sorry, I thought-"

"Never mind," I said, and turned back into the house, Julian and Genie Stacie behind me. God, did she need a bloody good hiding pronto.

"Oh, what a beautiful kitchen!" she exclaimed, running her hands over the black granite counter.

"Thank you. And this here is the hearth- it's really old but it works perfectly."

"Look at it! It's *huge*," Genie purred, batting her eyes at him to make sure he'd got her *double entendre*. I think even the hearth got it, along with every other inanimate object in there.

Julian coughed. "Well, er- Erica likes to cook and we often have guests. You could fit an entire cow in there, actually."

"Yes, you could fit *her* in there, too!" she pseudo-whispered to him with a giggle and pranced off. My jaw dropped. Again. I couldn't have heard correctly. There was no way an educated (?) woman would purposely offend her host. Right? I eyed the knife block on the counter, then her departing back and wondered if it was too late to take up knife-throwing as a hobby, using her narrow back as a target.

Julian cleared his throat and moved onto the living room, standing near the open fireplace. I glared at him, then at her, crossing my arms in front of my bovine udders, daring her to continue with her cow-comments.

And Julian- how dare he not even *try* to defend me! He continued his tour of the house so I had no choice but to follow them stonily around to the dining room where an old picture of a cow grazing in the

Tuscan countryside hung above the sideboard. I could only wait to see what kind of comment she'd come up with, but Julian steered her away from it as if it bore some more horrific truths about me that he couldn't deal with.

The fact that annoyed me most was that Genie Stacie in person was just as gorgeous as in the magazines. Maybe not as glamorous, but she had that old-world fragility to her. She was indeed a knockout. If anything, *I'd* gladly knock her out, teeth and all.

*

"What's the *matter* with you?" I demanded of Julian as we were getting ready for bed later that evening. The evening of our anniversary, in case you'd forgotten. And Genie had managed to squeeze an invitation for the night from us because by the time she'd finished demolishing my taste in decorating and pretty much my entire persona it was dark and Julian didn't want her on the roads at that hour. In fact, neither did I want her on the road. I preferred her at the bottom of a ditch, but no matter.

And now Julian stared at me blankly, surprised by my outburst.

"The 'cheap-looking linen' comment! What the hell does Genie Stacie know about tradition and the value of anything? Those linens were hand-embroidered by my grandmother! But most of all, the *roasted cow* comment! Why didn't you say anything?"

102

"Oh, that. She doesn't mean anything by it."

My eyes popped wide open. "Du-*uh*?'"

Julian shrugged. "Genie's like that. She's never liked to be exceeded in anything. It's just a weakness of hers."

"Exceeded? The woman called me a cow!"

"No, she didn't."

I gaped at him. "The woman suggested putting me in the *oven*!"

"To get rid of you as a rival, not because she sees you as a cow," he maintained.

"Rival?" I whispered. "Since when did she become my rival? Is there something I should know?"

Julian rolled his eyes. "That's not what I meant."

I grabbed my hips in my usual teapot gesture whenever I was furious. "Oh, but that's exactly what you meant!"

He sighed. "Stop it, Erica- you're exaggerating."

"Oh, I'd love to see *you*!" I threw back as I shimmied out of my jeans and left them there on the ground, along with my underwear and socks. If I was going to be seen as the family stable animal I might as well start acting like one.

Julian sighed, running a hand through his hair the way he did when he was frustrated, which was actually very rarely.

"Yes, Genie Stacie's not very tactful, but she was actually paying tribute to you."

"Tribute? Ha!" I snapped, pulling my nightgown over my head, too exhausted to shower. If our evening ablutions usually led to sex, tonight Julian was going to remain high and dry. Roasted cow, my foot.

"Of course. All these years she's always been the center of every man's attention, and now that she's seen that one man's attention focuses on his beloved wife, she goes all scared and tries to put herself up by bringing others down."

I threw back the covers and gave him my hairy eyeball before turning onto my side facing the wall. "Save your cheap psychology and your lame sugar-coating for an idiot. I'm not interested."

The bed creaked as he rolled over closer to me, and I could feel his face just above me although I was staring vehemently at one of my own Tuscan countryside paintings on the wall next to the window. And I wondered what *know-it-all* Genie Stacie would have to say about my painting technique. It was one of the first things I'd painted since we'd moved to Tuscany, when things were all hunky-dory and we were happy. Scratch that. When *I* was happy, because apparently everyone around me still was.

It turned out I wasn't so confident after all if I let a useless, shallow by-product of Hollywood get to me like this. Couldn't Julian see what she was?

"And did you see the way Maddy was staring at her?" I continued. Julian didn't answer. "What, are you sleeping already? I'm still talking to you!"

"I thought you'd said goodnight," he said.

"I didn't, actually."

"I noticed. I was just being sarcastic."

"Like your friend?" I broke off. "Already it's rubbed off on you?"

"Are we really arguing over Genie Stacie?" he pleaded.

"Did you or did you not see the effect she has on Maddy?"

"Actually, I saw the effect she had on *Warren*," Julian said and chuckled.

"You find this funny? We've got the queen of sleaze in our home and you *laugh*?"

"Oh, for God's sake, Erica. Lighten up, she's harmless."

"She's your blonde beauty, isn't she?" I asked louder than I'd intended.

He groaned. "Which blonde beauty are we talking about now?"

I crossed my arms over my chest. "The one with the Brazilian butt. Or is that another friend of yours that will be dropping in on us sometime soon?"

He exhaled sharply, as if I'd punched him, and let me tell you I wasn't far from it. "You went through my manuscript? I asked you to wait."

"Yeah, whatever," I muttered.

Julian turned in the bed. "That's not like you, is it?" he said softly, as if *he*'d been the offended one. Huh. "What's going on, Erica?" he asked, and suddenly I knew it wasn't just about the fact that I didn't have a Brazilian butt. The problem was that Genie Stacie did. Years of trying to build my self-confidence and now he comes up with this bloody penchant for Amazonian rear ends- what the *hell*?

"What made you do it?" he persisted, and I rolled my eyes.

"Oh, for Pete's sake. I was just curious. How the hell was I supposed to know I'd come face to face with your favorite kind of butt? And don't even think of denying it!"

Boy, was he mad now. "First of all, Erica, Genie Stacie is not the only blonde bombshell I've ever met. Second of all, that is purely fiction."

"Thirdly, I was attracted to her a long time ago. But then I got to know her and the attraction waned, because she was not the girl I thought."

"Meaning?"

He shrugged, still angry, and I knew he would be for a long time to come, but what the hell, I was much angrier than him.

"Meaning that she wasn't someone I could trust or depend upon. Someone like you, Erica."

I turned to face him, determined not to let him charm me, because that was the way our arguments ended, with me forgiving him.

"That's why I'm with you and not someone like her, sweetie," he murmured, bending over me, his forehead against mine. Uh-oh- I was falling for it.

"Get away from me," I snapped, pushing him away. "I don't trust you."

He exhaled, exhausted, poor guy. "Fine. Whatever. I'm going to sleep. Good night."

And so we slept, back to back, for the first time in eight years. There it was, hanging in the neutral airspace between us, heavy and humongous, my insecurity, back in all its glory.

CHAPTER NINE: Genie Stacie's Stay

Please don't ask me how or why, but harmless Genie Stacie's sleepover turned into a mini-vacation (for her) and I had to sit opposite her while she picked at lunch (she always slept through breakfast-time) and dinner, making brainless comments about everything.

Julian told her we were going to show her around and take her to the largest and oldest church in Siena, which had been erected (yes, he actually said *erected,* to which she smiled coyly at him) between the eleventh and twelfth century.

"Eleventh century, really?" she breathed, batting her baby blues at him. "Before or after Christ?" You see what I mean.

What didn't surprise me was that Maddy and Genie Stacie were in total sync and there was no way of putting a word in edge-wise. By day two they were like Siamese twins. Maddy had insisted on even sitting next to her during meals, simply glowing in the starlet's presence.

"You remind me of myself when I was youn- a *teenager*," Genie Stacie purred, reaching out to touch one of Maddy's curls. My daughter sat up in her chair and her eyes almost popped out of her head with pride.

"Really, Genie Stacie?" she breathed, incredulous at the divine grace bestowed upon her.

"Absolutely, sweetie. Only I started straightening my hair when I was fourteen."

"What on earth for?" I cut in, seeing where this was going. Julian gave me a sidelong glance and took a bite of his bread roll.

"Because straight hair is so much more *chic*. Look at Nicole Kidman."

"I *know*," Maddy agreed and I rolled my eyes.

Then she turned to me for the first time that morning. "Mom, can you drive me to Alessia's salon this afternoon? I want to get my hair permanently straightened."

"Ooh, no can do, sorry. We've got guests arriving later."

"I'll take her," volunteered Genie Stacie, who hadn't budged from the property- or Julian's side, for that matter, since she had darkened our doorstep.

Of course she either missed or ignored my eyebrows shooting up and down in a warning signal that only responsible parents can understand, the kind they use in the presence of their offspring when they don't want a particular subject to be mentioned. Instead Genie Stacie crossed her arms and beamed at me defiantly. So she wanted war? War it was.

I can tell you Julian saw the whole exchange, glanced at me, wiped his mouth and turned to our daughter. He knew how I felt about naturally curly hair and Maddy's obsessions about looking like a Barbie doll. "Sweetie, your hair is so beautiful, why ruin perfection?" he said.

I beamed at him and Maddy sighed. Genie Stacie had the decency to sit this one out. Or so I thought.

"Dad, you don't understand. I'd look really good with straight hair."

"You call Julian *Dad*...?" Genie whispered.

I put down my fork and shot her my hairy eyeball this time, but she didn't notice it because she was murmuring something and before I knew it she ran out of the kitchen.

"Uh, what the hell was that?" I asked, jerking my thumb towards the door.

Julian sighed. "Maddy, would you mind leaving us for a minute?"

"And miss out on a scoop? Are you, like, kidding me?"

"No he's not," I snapped, and Maddy rolled her eyes and took her glass of milk (soya, all of a sudden) into the living room.

Julian got to his feet and took our plates to the sink. I couldn't wait to hear it.

"Genie Stacie never had a father. Only a picture of him. I saw it. We look very similar."

"Oh, for Christ's sake, now she wants you to be her daddy, or better, her sugar daddy? Again?"

Julian sighed and ran his hands through his hair. If he kept this up he'd be bald by the time she left. Because she would be leaving soon. I prayed fervently, *Please let this tart be on her away ASAP, God. I beg of you.*

This whole Genie Stacie thing was affecting him (and me) more than I thought necessary. But then again, what did I know about their past relationship? Nothing, except for the selected excerpts he provided. And then it hit me.

"Did she lose your *baby* or something?"

I swear his eyes popped out of his head. "What? Of course not."

"Then what the hell is this all about, Julian? She comes here, starts directing my daughter, bats her baby blues at my twenty-year-old son-"

"That's not true, Erica. She just likes the kids."

"Oh, let me guess, she never had a brother or sister either, right?"

Julian frowned. "That's right, but there's no reason for you to be snarky. Yes, Genie Stacie is-"

I groaned, cutting him off. "Do you mind getting back on track here, please? I've got a busy day and I really don't want to spend it talking about Genie Stacie or worrying about what she's trying to do to my kids and husband."

"She's not trying to do anything. She's just a very lonely girl and as for the daddy comment, she always saw me as a kind of father figure and now I guess she's jealous."

"Father figure?" I giggled despite myself. Oh, the cheesiness of it all. "Is that what she would do to her father if she saw him, flirt with him in the hope of getting him in the sack again?"

Julian sighed, ran his hand through his hair yet again and started on the dishes. I got up and put myself between him and the sink. Something I rarely did.

"Ok, I'm sorry," I apologized. "Maybe that was uncalled for. But I hate having her here. She's obnoxious."

"I know. It won't last long. Three more days. I promise."

Three more days, for a total of one week. Was that how long her *win-Julian-back* plan was supposed to take? It had taken me *months* in Boston and still I wasn't sure. She, on the other hand, definitely had loads of self-confidence. And I found I had less and less each day.

"She wants you back- big time," I huffed.

"But I'm married," he said, leaning in to kiss me, pushing me back against the butler sink. "And in love. *Big time*."

"Yeah, yeah. Tell Genie Stacie that."

CHAPTER TEN: Goodnight Vienna

Gene Stacie was drawn to Julian like bees to honey. Only days ago she'd arrived on our doorstep with some crazy story about there being talks about Julian's novel becoming a movie and was he interested in writing the script? Also, she needed his help about something very delicate and only he would do. Meaning, probably, her zipper.

Butt out, I wanted to say to her. *We're trying to keep our family together and you're not helping.* Especially because whenever she was around Julian and I ended up arguing.

Don't get me wrong. I was thrilled for Julian. He deserved his novels to be made into a movie and more. But Genie Stacie could not be a condition. I realized that she had managed to make us argue just hours after she'd arrived with the news. She was talking to producers and one in particular (I can't remember his name because you could only believe half the stuff she said) was watching Julian's sales closely. Not that I didn't believe a producer was interested because Julian's books were beautifully written.

Genie Stacie had just- wait for it- *booked him a flight back with her to meet the producer.* Without even checking with him if it was okay. Evidently it was.

"What do you think?" he asked me when we were alone in our bedroom.

I shrugged, unable to believe he'd just shoot off at a moment's notice. "It sounds like a wonderful opportunity." *Gawd*, could I have been any more lame? *Support your man in all weathers*, I told myself, although it was storming brutally between us at the moment. Only a few hours ago he'd made an attempt to atone and now he was off again, in the arms of the cause of our fights, to boot. But I guess if it was all bone-fide then he had to give it a shot.

"If you think it's not a waste of time, by all means, go for it."

"I think I will. Good night," he simply answered and turned out the light. And good night Vienna.

*

The next day was Julian's forty-sixth birthday. I always wished I had more time between our anniversary and his birthday. I didn't do very well in the creative department so I always ended up flogging my brain for an original birthday gift, which never happened.

For the occasion Genie managed to surface before noon, wearing a barely-there burgundy dress, the same color of my *no-sex-I'm-on-the-rag-sheets*. I couldn't help but think that when Julian glanced at her he was thinking that her burgundy meant nothing *but* sex.

She flipped her platinum blonde hair so it rested all on one shoulder and flashed me a smile. The smile of a woman who knows she's prettier, sexier, richer and more successful than you. The smile of a woman who can steal your man in a heartbeat if she decides to. In my heart I already knew that was why she had 'dropped in' on us. In my heart I knew I had no chance, but somewhere a little atom of me hoped that Genie Stacie would be just a little scratch on the surface of our life. And boy, was I wrong.

Before I could produce my surprise gift from under the table, she whipped out a present like a rabbit out of a magic hat. I stared at her as Julian's face lit up in surprise.

"What's this?" Julian asked. As if he didn't know.

"You don't think I forgot your Burberry day, do you?"

Burberry, for those of you who didn't know, was Julian's favorite designer, being British and all that. But Burberry *day*? Please kill me now.

"Ah, Genie, you didn't have to-" he lied, and I wanted to clobber him over the head with my stupid gift.

"Nonsense! I always liked buying you presents, remember? Now let's see how it fits!"

And, as God is my witness, before my very eyes she dived for the edge of his T-shirt (the one with *I love Siena* on it, my first present to him in Tuscany) and yanked it up his body and over his head with hardly a protest from him. They so obviously had done this thousands of times before. Before he was married to me, one hopes.

"You're as ripped as you always were, you Fox!" she said as she patted his lower abs, too close to south for my comfort. Then she helped him into a beautiful, I have to say, beige cashmere sweater.

I coughed. I didn't mean to, because part of me wanted to see how far Julian would let her go, while the rest of me wanted to punch him and pull Genie Stacie's straight blonde hair out of her dark curly roots. Then she turned to me as if she'd suddenly remembered we were in the real world and not her own personal dream and said, beaming, "Fox was his nickname on the team."

"Uh-huh," I said, clutching the measly Polo shirt I'd bought him, this time a bright blue (I had already gone through the gamut of greens ranging from pale aquamarine to dark green over eight years of birthdays, Christmases and Valentine's days). Ok, so I wasn't very original with gifts, but it wasn't as if I *always* bought him Polo shirts. I also bought him sweaters, trousers or swimsuits, according to the season. What the heck was he going to need a sweater for in the summer? At least my gifts were ready for use. And so was she, judging by the way she swayed from side to side.

And then, out of the blue, I could just *feel* my marriage shaking.

*

"What a bunch of crap," Judy scoffed when I related my fears to her. "The guy's all eyes for you,

Erica! Don't you remember me making fun of you two? You're both so gooey-sweet!"

We were? Damn right we were. But those words, "Brazilian butt" made me all the more conscious of my round chin, the lack of bony or sharp edges on me and *my* not-so-Brazilian butt. Is that what he wanted? Between that and the leggy blonde I was out.

Just like eight years ago, Julian could have anyone- even if she would moan "Oh, sì!" instead of "Oh, yes!" now that we were living in Tuscany. And after having accepted that it was me he wanted, why did it hurt to read about his ideal (and unrealistic) woman? I mean, come on. I was his wife, his rock, his companion. She was just a little tart he'd had while he was a baseball star and too young to know any better.

"Besides," Judy continued, yanking me back from self-pity, "all men dream of a Brazilian butt and a leggy blonde."

I knew that was true, but Julian had always been so sweet and passionate *only* with me, I'd almost forgotten that he was, at the end of the day, a hot-blooded man in his mid-forties. Damn. That was it- a mid-life crisis!

"Steve confessed something to me once," Judy said as she lit a cigarette. "He said he loved me but he needed more variety."

"You're not thinking of pulling a threesome, are you?" I asked, bewildered.

"If that's what it takes to keep my man interested…"

I imagined myself and Julian, plus Genie Stacie all in the same bed, and I wanted to laugh. And then I wanted to cry, because I pictured the two of them, both statuary in their beauty, a twirl of vanilla and cinnamon, (Julian was very dark now) lost in the throes of passion, and me taking up half the bed with my un-Brazilian butt, waiting for my turn, because there'd be no way I could ever compete with Genie Stacie.

"You don't understand, Judy. Julian seems to have this soft spot for her. He forgives everything she does or says, even if it hurts me."

"Yeah?" was all she said.

"Yeah. Is that normal?"

"Not really, no. Maybe it's for old times' sake."

For some reason Judy had shifted from supporting me to supporting my fears and my ears pricked up.

For old times' sake? Just how important had Genie Stacie been to him? *Good enough for a roll in the hay important*, or *I want you to be with you forever* important? Well, neither of those scenarios were an option any longer if I could help it.

*

Later that day, as I was rolling out the dough for home-made ravioli, alongside a pot of Shepherd's Pie, (he was still a Brit at heart) I had the horrible idea of glancing out the window onto the patio.

There, in our very own private pool, the one that was used solely by Julian, the kids and I and our personal friends, was Genie Stacie, floating idly.

Julian was in one of the loungers doing some paperwork, totally oblivious as he always was when working.

Genie Stacie was talking and laughing and Julian put his binder aside to smile at her, but I could see it was a polite smile and nothing more. She said something and laughed and when her bikini top magically slipped out of place, she simply whipped it off and threw it onto the side. Even from where I was watching, I saw Julian's back straighten before he jumped to his feet and left her there.

Needless to say I was fuming at this tramp's gall. But I was also proud of my gentleman. It wasn't every day that a guy walked away from a bare-breasted Genie Stacie.

Alone and defeated, Genie Stacie reached for her bikini top again as I watched. What I hadn't calculated was Julian coming back through the kitchen doors.

"Hey, babe," he breathed, blocking my view of Genie Stacie through the window. "Can I help you cook lunch?" he asked, probably trying to re-balance his karma. Even if he'd behaved in a gentlemanly way, he was probably still shaken by Genie Stacie's free show.

I turned to face him. "You can move out of the way now. She put it back on."

Julian stared at me, blanching, raising his hands in protestation, an explanation already forming on his lips.

"It's okay, honey," I assured him. "I saw the way she cornered you. *Now* will you believe me?"

He closed his mouth and nodded.

I handed him some potatoes. "Peel these for me, will you?"

He took them from me as if they were precious stones. "I love you, Erica," he growled softly.

I reached up and caressed his jaw. "If you love me now wait until you taste this Shepherd's Pie."

*

At ten o'clock the next morning Maddy and Genie Stacie came down the stairs together, twin gaits and dressed almost the same, refusing breakfast and hustling out the door.

"Maddy" I called. "Just where are you going?"

My daughter rolled her eyes and sighed, throwing a "Shopping, remember?" over her shoulder. "In Florence. Back tonight."

"Florence? But Maddy, I thought we-"

"Don't worry, Erica, it's on me!" Genie Stacie sing-songed as they left, arm in arm. The shopping in Florence, I remembered very well. It was supposed to have been a chic treat for my daughter and myself. I'd half-pinned my hair up like I did on special occasions and even dressed up in my sequined turquoise dress with the daring neckline Maddy approved so much of. Today she didn't even notice.

I took off my fancy shoes, my feet already thanking me, and threw my car keys onto the side table, staring after them as Genie's Lamborghini sped down the hill, the wide wheels gripping the old, winding roads. My daughter in the passenger seat of an expensive sports car driven by a raging idiot who thought sixteen year-old girls should be on the pill just in case they met someone one night. What a sight.

I secretly blamed Julian for this blonde airhead that had found her way to our front door. And into our daughter's head. But enough was enough. When they got home I'd have to bring them both down a notch or two.

But when they finally did make it through the front door I almost screamed. My daughter's head looked like it had been forcefully wedged through a crack in the front door.

"What have you done to your hair?" I cried, my hands flying to my mouth as I looked upon my daughter who looked like something between Marcy (who always straightened her hair even now that it was thinning) and

Genie Stacie, only a much younger, clueless (if possible) version.

"I straightened it!" Maddy cried back triumphantly. "Doesn't it look, like, awesome?"

"No, it *doesn't!*" I moaned as Julian came through the door and stopped dead in his tracks, his eyes huge at the sight of his daughter's squashed head.

"That's nothing compared to the gorgeous clothes I got her!" Genie Stacie cried, like she was about to break into tears with the sheer joy of it. "Maddy, show your mother and Julian what I bought you," she urged as she dropped her designer bags and skipped to the bar in the corner and poured herself a Martini, Marcy's favorite drink. Anybody see a pattern here?

"Look, Julian!" Maddy casually addressed her step-father as she pulled out from a bag with the words D&G on it a strip of black cloth smaller than my cloth duster. I didn't know what was worse- what I'd heard or what I was looking at. I stared, wordless.

And my man, who'd coughed at the sight of the mini-outfit, didn't miss a beat. "Young lady, when did you stop calling me 'Dad'?

"Isn't it gorgeous?" Genie Stacie squealed and Maddy joined her, and soon they were stomping their dainty little feet against the terracotta tiles as if they badly needed to go to the bathroom.

"Sexy, isn't it?" Maddy prompted as she put it against herself. Julian stood up, his face tight. "Uhm, Genie Stacie, can I have a word with you in the living room?"

Genie Stacie looked in my direction, satisfied, inflating her chest under Julian's blinking gaze. "Of course, Fox," she purred, sashaying before him.

Fox? I stared at them, then back at my sixteen-year-old. Did she just say *sexy*? To the man that used to play in the sandbox with her and teach her how to kick a ball? To the man that told her bedtime stories and tucked her in? Maddy had *always* referred to Julian as *Dad* until now. What kind of garbage was this peroxide flake piling into my daughter's head?

"Maddy, why did you call your father by his Christian name?" I asked her the second the door closed.

"Genie Stacie said Julian's not my real father," Maddy shrugged.

"Yes, well we didn't need her to tell us that, did we now?"

"I know, Mom, but Julian is really only twenty-seven years older than me."

I raised my eyebrows at her. Maybe Genie Stacie could marry an old man like Tom Jackson but my daughter was doing no such thing. "Only?"

"Look at Genie Stacie. Tom Jackson is thirty-five years older than her."

124

"Yeah, and look how that ended."

Maddy sighed wistfully. "I want someone older than me, too. I'm sick and tired of these young pups."

Young *pups*? "Maddy, you are to stop this nonsense now. And you are returning these things immediately."

"Mom- no!"

"Maddy- *yes*."

"But they're so beautiful!"

I sighed. "Yes, they are, Maddy, but "Not on my sixteen-year-old daughter, they're not."

"You're just jealous!" she spat in fury. "*Jealous*! Because she is gorgeous and famous and men all over the world are crazy about her, including Dad!"

I know it must have taken me a few minutes to close my mouth, because nothing I could say would do my thoughts justice. So I settled on being me. "Alright, that's enough! Go to your room. I'm having these, thank you," I said, taking the bags of designer postage-stamp-sized couture from her.

All men including Dad. Was I so blind I couldn't see what was sitting astride my nose, mocking me?

"I know, I know- please don't say anything," Julian said, holding his hand up as he came into our bedroom later that night. "I think I got through to Genie Stacie though."

"Thank you," I said. "You see what I'm talking about?"

"Oh yeah." He sat down on his side of the bed with his back to me and pulled off his socks.

"And?" I prompted.

"And she says she's sorry. She'll never do it again."

"Damn right she won't, because she's finally leaving."

"Erica... Genie Stacie is very fragile."

"Then she can go to a shrink like I did, Julian. All that matters to me is my family. It was supposed to be just a short visit and she's invaded our home and our privacy, not to say turned my daughter against me."

"She hasn't turned her against you..."

"You think? Maddy won't talk to me because I won't let her wear those three stitches that Genie Stacie chose for her."

"Calm down, Erica..."

"No, I can't and I won't calm down, Julian. I have a sixteen year-old daughter to raise, don't you *understand?*"

"*We* have a sixteen year-old daughter to raise," he corrected me as he pulled off the rest of his clothes in one swing and stood up, naked.

Damn, I'd never get over how gorgeous he was. And he was, until it was irrefutably proven otherwise, all mine. I instantly felt like an impostor sitting at a queen's banquet, dreading the moment someone would catch me out and take him away from me.

Yeah, I know I sound nuts, but you try living with him and Genie Stacie under the same roof for a week. Deep inside I couldn't blame women for admiring him, but I damn well could do so for them trying to steal him.

I watched as he strode into the bathroom, turned on the shower and brushed his teeth, ignoring me now. Which caught my attention big-time. He *never* did that. Ok, so he was mad. I had exaggerated. But certainly a little argument wasn't going to keep us from... atoning? The shower was our make-up place. In view of this we had had a mega-shower built with a seating ledge. Worked like a charm.

As he stepped in and began to lather his hair I pulled at the buttons of my nightgown. But when I got under the jets next to him, he kept his eyes closed, as if he didn't want to see me, let alone make up. "I've decided I'm going to the States with Genie Stacie tomorrow to meet this producer. Don't bother driving me. I'll hitch a lift from her."

CHAPTER ELEVEN: Secret Loves and Love Secrets

The next morning, to add insult to injury, I got my period. So much for IVF. No worries- it hardly ever worked the first time, right?

Downstairs in the kitchen Julian eyed me, threw a glass of orange juice down his throat, kissed the top of Maddy's still sleek head, patted Warren on the back and headed towards the front drive where Genie Stacie was already tooting her horn, probably because she was dying to get past the first bend in the road and out of view to jump into his lap.

But at the door Julian turned to look at me, waiting for me to kiss him. All I wanted to do was throw my arms around him and tell him that IVF had been a failure. But I couldn't bring myself to give him yet another reason to be disappointed by me. Besides, I was still mad at him. Even more now, as if the IVF disaster was his fault. Deep down I felt it was, because if he had never come up with this crazy request for a child I would never have been bothered that I couldn't give him one.

"Have a great time," I said through clenched teeth, mostly for the kids' benefit. Fact was I wanted him to have a horrible time with Genie Stacie. I wanted her to get air sick and puke on his trousers. And he'd be stuck with Smellie Stacie all the way over the Atlantic.

Maddy and Warren stared back and forth between us. They were used to kisses and hugs and all sorts of mushy stuff between us. But somehow, in the space of a week, that had all changed. I had turned from loving to resentful, while Julian had turned from sweet to impatient and distant.

But now Julian cocked his head at me, halfway between hurt and wanting to say, *Come on, sweetie- it's still me, your loving husband Julian.* Only he didn't actually say it, but the look on his face was enough for me. And so I flew into his arms, burying my face into his shoulder as he squeezed me tight.

"That's more like it," Warren murmured and Maddy snorted. The fact that she cheered for my rival to break up our family was unforgiveable. I turned in Julian's embrace and sent her a warning look. While good old Warren had always been faithful, I realized I had to win my daughter back from the Shallow World of the Paper Dolls. And after her I still *wanted* kids?

"Have a safe trip," I whispered as we walked through the front door, still a tangle of arms and hands, towards Genie Stacie chomping at the bit in her Lamborghini.

"Take care, honey, and please be happy in the meantime, okay?" he whispered, and I swallowed hard and nodded.

"Don't worry, I'll take super-extra care of him," my nemesis chimed and before I could blink she drove my husband off our property and away from me.

I drifted upstairs and put my burgundy sheets on the bed. Even if Julian wasn't there, I needed a reminder that I wasn't going to have any sex this week, and as per the mathematical Transitive Property, neither was he.

**

"Hi Sweetie," came Julian's deep warm voice over the phone and immediately that Julian-shaped place inside my heart tingled with warmth. He'd been gone one day and I *missed* him.

"Julian…" I breathed, half-expecting he'd forget to call. "How was the flight?"

Julian groaned. "Gruesome. Genie Stacie was sick all over me."

Was I a witch or what? What had started on my behalf as a dainty, controlled giggle turned out into a big healthy belly laugh. "Oh, Julian, that's horrible!"

He chuckled. "I've had a shower but I still can't get the smell out of my nose."

As much as that was ungentlemanly, I loved him for it.

"How are the kids?" he asked.

"Warren's in his room studying."

"Without Stefania?"

"Without Stefania."

"Wow."

"And Maddy's out with Angelica."

"Again?" School was out and the two were relatively free to rampage around town. I was confident, with eyes everywhere on them from Renzo, owner of the bakery-café, to our butcher, baker and even the candlestick maker (I'm not being funny).

There was nowhere they could go (they weren't allowed outside of Castellino without our permission, Angelica's mom agreed with us on that long ago) without being seen. We had them practically tagged like two little bunnies.

"And oh, and Maddy still hates me."

"No, she doesn't. Hug them both for me, will you?"

"Oh, I don't think I can get that close to her."

Julian laughed and I suddenly really wanted him home next to me.

"Look, sweetie, Terry's due in a minute and I have to finish getting dressed. Talk tomorrow, okay?"

"Is Genie Stacie with you?"

"What?"

Me and my big mouth. "I mean, in the same hotel."

"Of course not. She went home."

"Did you find out what it was that she needed you for? The problem that only you could solve?"

"Uh, kind of. I'll tell you about it when I get back."

"Tell me now."

I heard Julian call, "It's open," and then Terry Peterson's loud booming voice, "Hey, Fox, you ready to hit the town?"

"Ah," I said, resenting the man from even this far. "Okay, Julian, have a good time."

"I'm meeting a producer for dinner," he said softly. Apologetically, almost.

"Great!" I said. "Good luck, then."

"Love you, sweetheart."

"Me, too! Bye!" and I hung up before he could answer.

Not that I cared about Terry Peterson constantly being on the prowl- that was his business. I trusted Julian. But how the hell was I going to sleep, wondering why Genie Stacie had elected Julian as her only savior? Why was he the only one who could help her?

I pretty much trudged through the next few days without him, preparing meals, directing Caterina the housekeeper with our changeover days and guests and meeting up with Renata for lunch.

"Where's that husband of yours gone, to the States again?" she asked over our Pasta alla Carbonara.

"Uh-huh."

"With that flaky blonde?"

"Renata, please don't rub it in. I'm pissed off enough as it is."

"Shut up. Tell me all!"

So I did. Marco was away on business, only without a blonde. My kids played with Renata's younger ones as we enjoyed a bottle of *vino rosso* and each other's company. Warren was fake-wrestling with Matteo, Renata's eight year-old, while Maddy had momentarily shed her princess aura and was braiding stunningly beautiful twelve year-old Chiara's (who had a crush on Warren) long black hair.

Renata's glass clinked against mine. "So what are we toasting?" she asked.

I shrugged. "My imminent divorce?"

"Don't be ridiculous, Erica! Your husband loves you. Not even a Hollywood ex flame can take him away from you. You are a *family*."

She was a great gal, Renata. Perhaps a tad too naïve?

"Yeah, I like to think so, too, but you should see the way even Maddy was on my case," I whispered. "I think she likes Genie Stacie more than she likes me."

Renata chuckled and shook her head. "Silly. You are the most likeable woman there is. And besides, Maddy doesn't count- she's a teenager, an unreliable species."

I grinned at her and nodded. "See, Renata? That's why I love you so much. You always take the drama out of everything."

She took my hand and smiled. "You will be fine. Your family is safe. Don't let a paper doll scare you."

Paper doll. Just the term I'd used for Genie Stacie.

*

As I was down in the front garden giving my brand new (and hunky) gardener Piero instructions, the phone rang. I reached into my pocket.

"Hello?"

"Hi honey, sorry- bad news. I'm going to have to cancel my flight home," Julian said from the other side of the Atlantic Ocean.

"A producer wants me to meet some more people."

From behind me Piero, my new gardener, appeared on the door holding a new rosebush I wanted planted.

"Erica, how do you like this- is it big enough for you?"

"Who's that?" Julian said.

I covered the mouthpiece but it was too late. "Uh, that was our new gardener, Piero."

Silence.

And then, to make things worse while trying to make them better, I explained, or tried to. "He's working on my bush. My rosebush."

"He's *what*?"

Silence again on the other end as I could hear him trying to make sense of it and it wasn't looking good.

"You mean you're meeting more movie producers?" I asked, trying to get the conversation back to safer ground. "That's great, Julian!"

"You hired a gardener without even telling me? I thought I was in charge of your bush," he added.

Yeah, so did I. "You *were* in charge. And you did a great job. But you're never around anymore, and my bush needs tending to."

Okay, this was getting farcical. "I'm not good with plants, you know that. Remember my succulents on the windowsill in Boston? Remember how you kept them from dying?"

"Erica, what the hell?"

"Are you jealous?" I asked hopefully.

"Bloody right I am," he swore, his Liverpudlian accent at its most obvious when he was angry, which was very rare.

"Good. I'm sorry, but you were away. I needed the job done. Be thankful I wasn't horny instead."

Dead silence.

"Ok, that was a joke."

I heard him sigh loudly. "You could have at least let me know what was going on."

Piero looked at me expectantly. "I'll be with you in a minute, Piero. Honey, I have to go. Piero needs me."

"*Piero, honey*? What the hell is going on there?"

"No, I said Piero, full-stop. *Then* I said honey. To you."

"We'll talk about this when I get home," Julian said, rather teed off.

Good. It served him right. If he could have Genie Stacie, I could have Piero. I wondered how we had managed to start this silly *I'll-show-you* game. Although it was childish, it made me feel better. For about two minutes.

Had Julian jacked me up so much with how great I was all these years that the minute he was away I needed male attention? Shouldn't it have been the opposite- that Julian had jacked me up so much I actually didn't *need* any more attention? Was I at the point where I needed a man to keep me uplifted? Whatever happened to *me,* the old Erica Cantelli? Got depressed and lost her confidence while trying to have a baby, that's what happened.

Ah, but not for long! Because I could do this! Keep my man *and* give him a baby, no matter what Dottoressa Bardotti said- for all she knew, I could get pregnant in a few weeks' time. The next day I went out and got some more stinging nettles.

*

One week later Julian was home. He'd met the right people, established contacts, was waiting to hear now. Didn't want to elaborate as he was tired. And mad at me because of Piero.

At that point I daren't tell him about the IVF failure either. Because he seemed less sympathetic, less worried and probably more concerned with other matters. He kissed me hard, almost angrily, as if he wanted to get back at me for the gardener and my bush joke when he happened to look out the window to where said gardener, dressed only in a pair of teeny tiny shorts, was washing his heavenly bod under the outdoor shower.

We both watched as the Adonis shook his wet mane and rubbed his face. He was indeed something to look at. He also looked like I'd planted him there and then with a script, *barely clad hunk stretches his fab bod under the water jets in slow motion.* Well, let's be honest. I could've hired Mr. Alessi, Renata's elderly gardener. But he didn't look anything like Piero. Even a straight man like Julian had to admit it.

"Bloomin' *heck*- is that him? Where'd you find him, in an issue of- never mind."

"Good, isn't he? I mean, he's *very* dedicated. Won't go home until he's finished the job." (If you detect the sarcasm in my voice, I can assure you that Julian did, too, only he preferred not to rise to the bait. He really was a gentleman. Most of the time. I was the woman who could turn a saint into a psychopath. Or so Julian often said.)

His mouth clamped shut as he turned away from the window. "Right."

I, for one, was super-cool. "So tell me more about your movie talks?"

"Not now." And with that he plunked his bottle onto the counter and picked up his suitcase from where he left it, throwing his laundry into the washer. Shirts, trousers, socks, briefs.

Shit. I had some major Damage Control to do here. "Tell you what. Why don't we go upstairs and have a nice shower?" *Which was code for, Let's have sex and forget about the whole thing, yes?*

To which he readily responded, "I'm too angry right now," while snapping the washer door shut and brushing past me. "I'm going for a ride."

Later hat evening Julian made an unexpected appearance in the bedroom. Which was a big thing, considering I thought he would sleep in the guestroom. Instead, he lay next to me in silence, as if waiting for me to say something. Well, he'd have a long wait. He was the one that had acted like an idiot. It was up to him to apologize.

But after several minutes had passed by and still not a word I turned my head towards him. He was sweating and breathing shallowly. I whipped to my knees.

"Julian? What's wrong?"

Silence.

"Julian- are you okay?"

He finally groaned, ever so softly.

"Talk to me? What happened?"

"I went for a ride…"

"Yes?"

"No saddle..." he rasped. "I'm bruised... down there..."

"You went *horse*-riding without a saddle? What are you trying to do, play Tarzan?" I ran into the bathroom, giggling hysterically, and returned with a cold washcloth.

"Here, let me have a look," I whispered, and he winced.

"It's not a pretty sight," he warned me.

I looked up. "Trust me, it never was."

Despite the pain, he chuckled, then coughed and winced, all in one breath.

"It serves you right," I said as I lay the cloth on him and ran downstairs to get some ice, an ice bucket and a bottle of our own champagne which I hid under the bed. With a relationship like ours, you never knew how the evening might develop.

"How could you be so stupid to ride off without a saddle?" I asked as I wrapped the ice in a washcloth and placed it on his disaster area.

"I was- ouch- angry."

"Yes, you made that quite clear."

I wiped his sweaty forehead, my fingers light on his skin, his hair damp. He turned his head so our eyes met. "I'm sorry to have been such a wanker," he moaned. "I should've known better."

"I'm sorry too. Especially now. IVF tanked."

He reached up to caress my face. "Sweetie… why didn't you tell me?"

I shrugged, blinking back the tears. "Is this injury going to put the project on hold? Or am I getting ahead of myself? I mean, you don't want out of the baby project, do you?"

"Erica…"

"I won't force you into doing anything you don't want, Julian."

He grinned. A half, painful grin. "You mean like you usually do?"

"What are you talking about?"

"Oh, well, let's see. The thermal vests I have to wear in the winter or you have a sulk? Or the vegetables you pile into me?"

"But I'm just trying to take care of you…"

"Honey, if I got this far without you mothering me to death, I think I have a chance of surviving without your cauliflower."

"Right. Got it."

"You're not offended?"

"Only if you don't turn around and tell me you don't love me anymore."

He stared at me, trying to sit up. "Erica, please. You have to stop this madness. You're behaving like a teenager."

"No, I'm being practical. Say you wanted a divorce. Would you tell me?"

He groaned. "I'd have to, wouldn't I?"

"Just answer my question, will you?"

He sighed. "Listen to me, and listen good. I don't want a divorce. Yes, recently you're being a real pain in the arse, but this is just a bad spell and it will all go away once you understand Genie Stacie has no hold whatsoever over me."

Huh. "And what about the baby? Do you still want one?"

He looked me in the eye. "Do you?"

This game was getting old. "I asked you first."

"I don't want to put any pressure you. If it never happens- and I'm speaking on a hypothetical level- it's okay. As long as I have you and the kids. You are more important than a pregnancy that might only be in our fantasies. Now how's that for an answer?"

"Bloody good. So all this time you haven't been ignoring me? Hoping I wouldn't get pregnant?"

He cocked his head at me as if to say, *get real, will you?*

"I just wish that you would talk to me instead of inventing twisted scenarios in that maniac mind of yours," he breathed as I flipped the cold cloth over. "Ouch, easy, babe."

I smiled down at him. He hadn't called me that in a long time. I was glad *I* was still his babe instead of a dumb blonde with long legs.

"How do you put up with me?" I asked as I nuzzled his neck.

He looked at me and I could tell he was half way between confused and impatient himself. My poor Julian who had the patience of Job. "Just tell me what's really bothering you, Erica."

Ouch. Ack. "I hate not being in control of my life- of this... *baby* thing," I whispered, surprising even me. My shrink in Boston would have applauded me.

At that, he groaned. "Honey- let go a little. You are in control of practically everything else."

"I am," I nodded, then looked up. "I'm sorry. I'm bossy, I know."

"That's okay. I like you that way."

"You do?" I knew he did, but I just liked hearing it.

"Hell, yes. You're an absolute control freak but that's fine because I like the way you like things too."

I felt my eyes pop. "Yeah?"
"Of course."

Wow. "Wait- what do you mean- am I really really that much of a control freak?"

Julian unfolded his arms (good sign) and sighed, taking me by the shoulders and speaking softly the way you do to a mental case.

"Sweetie- yes. You are a complete war chief." He grinned, and I knew everything was okay again.

*

The next morning, after a night with his rocks on the rocks, we had a good session of hard (but careful) love and came down the next morning hand in hand like two teenagers who couldn't keep their hands off each other.

"How about an espresso?" I offered as he kissed me. "Not that you need any waking up."

"*Sì, grazie,*" he said with a grin and I reached for the mocha on the top shelf as he answered the house phone.

"What the hell, man, your cell is off," thundered Terry's voice over the phone, loud and clear. Jesus, I'd get a new phone system just so I didn't have to hear the jerk. "I get you Marty Liebermann, the best producer in Hollywood and you won't even *meet* the man because your *dog* is having surgery?"

Julian glanced at me, his ears turning pink, then stepped away as his hand stole to the back of his neck like whenever he was embarrassed.

"It's true," Julian lied, now scrubbing his nape.

"It has to be! I've never heard of anything so ridiculous!"

"Terry, I've got to go, I'll call you later, ok?"

And before Terry could bark back an answer, Julian hung up with a sigh of relief.

I put my hands on my hips tea-pot style and looked at him. "Susie is no spring chicken anymore, but she's hardly at that stage, is she? What's going on, Julian?"

Julian shrugged. "I just needed to stay home for a bit, that's all."

"And you turned down a meeting with a Hollywood producer? *Why?*"

"It doesn't matter anymore, Erica. Really. Where's that espresso you promised me?"

I stared down at the mocha that was still in my hands and tried to twist it open.

"Here, let me do that, sweetie," Julian said as he took it from me, unscrewed the top and filled the bottom with cold water and kissed me on the lips so tenderly I wanted to cry. He'd done it to be home with me at such a tough time for me. I mean for *us*. And then I understood I had to stop playing goddess, or my version of it.

"Call Terry back to tell him you're going to meet Marty Lieberstein."

"Liebermann."

"Liebermann. Now go. I'll bring your espresso into your study. I don't want you making more sacrifices than necessary for me, Julian. Go."

He looked at me longingly and kissed me again as I packed the coffee down tight so it would come out nice and strong, just the way he liked it, while a million questions roiled around in my mind. I had to stop being a control freak and let things be as they were.

I decided right there and then I was going to change, resign from my pseudo-position of Goddess in Charge- effective immediately. My heart felt like it was coming out of my ears but hey- this was a new, better me. A stronger me.

*

Exactly two days after Julian departed for the US to speak to Marty Liebermann, Renata was clumping up our stone staircase in her crocs, carrying her favorite raffia grocery bag. She took one look at me and grunted.

"Sorry about the IVF," she said as she slipped into the chair opposite me.

I sighed. "Why do you think it's not working, Renata? What am I doing wrong?"

Renata poured me a tall glass of iced tea, then one for herself, slipping slowly. "*Oyoy*, it's because you're as strung as a bow- look at you, shoulders almost to your ears. Just trust him. Be supportive and patient. Here," she said, plunking the bag down before me.

I sat up a bit higher. "What's that?"

Renata smiled. "This is my especially designed for you baby-making kit."

"Oh-kay." I laughed, but she was serious.

"Just listen to me, Erica. You have to look at the problem objectively. You and Julian want a baby but no luck so far, yes?"

I crossed my arms in front of my chest. I didn't have the time for the, as Julian always says, *Bleeding Obvious*, nor the will for a recap of my failures.

But she was on a mission, and with that glint in her eye that only promised mischief. "Let's see, where is it? Ah, *sì*- here, look!"

A candle? "What am I going to do with this?"

But she was already pulling out other objects: lavender oil, a CD, feathers, a silk scarf and a bottle.

"Forget Genie Stacie. This is aromatherapy."

I rolled my eyes. "I know what it's for, but you think a nice smell and a flame is going to make her go away? Or make my eggs attractive?"

"This is not about your eggs. This is about... *communion*."

Not that New Age and ancient Chinese medicine stuff again? "Communion," I repeated bluntly.

Boy, sometimes I wonder how Renata even managed to get a business degree. Sometimes she looked so unworldly it just didn't fit her practical mothering and cooking and yes, *wifing*. She put her man and her kids above everything else just like I did. At times we were like twin souls, but today? Nope.

"Here's what you do," she said. "When he gets back, you send the kids to my place-"

"Renata..."

But she only raised her voice above mine- "-*and* you cook his favorite dinner. No restaurant- it's too distracting. You need to be completely alone."

I opened my mouth but shut it again at the look on her face. Boy, she was good.

"After dinner, you leave the leftovers and dishes on the table- you'll need them later- and then you entice him upstairs with that look."

"What look?"

She smiled. "The look that every man recognizes- it's universal, yet everyone has their own."

"Right."

"Light the candle while you are both undressing-"

"Who says we undress?" I quipped.

"Erica- do you want this baby or not?" she scolded me and I sobered instantly.

"Sorry. Go on."

"Use anything and everything in this kit to stimulate each other's senses. It's not about sex. It's about *connecting*- feeling the other. It's a joining of two souls, not just two bodies, you know."

I groaned inwardly. Time to dig out my mini-Kamasutra? I might have even thrown it away. Julian and I didn't need it. We were completely happy with each other. And yet... you never knew. Was there a baby-making section I'd missed?

"Just take your time, Erica. Don't think of how many times you're doing it- just think of how much you enjoy each other's company, in and out of the bed."

"Got it."

"And... start taking this every morning on an empty stomach." She produced a glass bottle full of some green cloudy liquid. Stinging nettles again?

"Aloe Vera," she pronounced it *Alloway Vayra*. This will clean your system completely of all toxins and," she shrugged, "who knows? You might have a *bambino* on the way this time next month."

Fat chance. Still...

I unscrewed the cap and sniffed suspiciously. "This thing has booze in it."

"Just a little. In order to expedite the waste quicker."

"I've never heard of such crap..."

"You won't even try it?"

"Damn right I will."

She grinned. "Good. Drink a half espresso-cup full every morning. It should last you about a month. I've got some more where that came from."

"Thanks."

"You're welcome. And one more thing."

"Yeah?"

"Have *fun- it's not a chore!*"

It made sense, though. Lately it did feel like a chore. Not that we didn't enjoy it, but Julian seemed to think that reading the same script over and over again made us learn our lines better. Well, it didn't because the whole time lately I'd be thinking about the baby, imagining my teeny tiny egg venturing out of an ovary, hoping to meet a pack of his swimmers and hoping the best would sink his teeth into it.

Just how much did we women hurt ourselves, hoping and imagining too much when we should just relax and sing *Que sera, sera*, whatever will be, will be? But of course you know me, the supreme control freak. I could never relax and sing to that tune.

If anything I wasn't pissed off anymore. Now I was intrigued. If Renata the baby-maker had a baby-making kit for me, my gut told me to accept it. With thanks. Even if I didn't believe in miracles anymore. So I made a cup of good strong, *No-sleeping-tonight coffee*. I knew *I'd* need it.

*

With Julian gone during the few days of my blue window, I decided to forget about baby-making for the moment and concentrate on not what I didn't have, but what I could lose if we didn't reconnect pronto. And so began my winning-him-back strategy.

I'd surprise him when he returned with an improvised trip to the Apuan Alps, far from indiscreet eyes. And with a little number I'd found in an *Intimeria* in Siena. A pair of knickers, to be exact.

So what, you might think. Ah, but these knickers were special. Incredible. Well, to be precise, they were edible. In fact, they were completely made of chocolate.

All I can reveal is that the next night, when I saw a taxi coming up our cypress tree-lined entrance, I'd speed-dialed our babysitter Giulia who (having been fore-warned) showed up just as I kissed Julian and showed him our packed luggage.

As the Jeep climbed high up into the hills to get to his 'surprise' I lifted my legs on the dashboard with the oldest trick in the world of my stockings having a run in them.

"You never wear stockings," he observed as his eyes darted to my legs which, I have to say, didn't look that bad from this angle. Had the rice cakes and carrot sticks finally started to work their magic?

I rubbed my calves gently, up and down and again his eyes darted to my legs.

"Hello," he drawled.

Yes!

"Hello yourself," I whispered huskily. "I bought a new bra while you were away…"

In the penumbra, I saw him swallow, steal me the sexiest look I'd ever seen, and drag his eyes back to the road which was twisting and turning up the mountain now. Perhaps this was not a great idea. Maybe I should wait until-

"Aren't you going to show me?" he whispered.

Ooh, good, he was hanging off the edge of his seat now.

"I might. But can you handle it, with these curves?" I quipped. His eyes twinkled at my double-entendre, the sap. Was there one guy on the planet that had an ounce of discipline?

"Babe- I know your curves better than anything," he drawled.

"Ah, but there's always something new to discover," I whispered, moving in closer to lick the side of his neck. He shivered and murmured, "Get away from me, you minx..."

I laughed- as throatily as I could, mind you- as my hand touched his thigh. I didn't need to go there or turn on the overhead light to see he was... intrigued.

What guy could resist any kind of foreplay?

When we finally arrived, he came to a stop, his breath ragged.

At the end of the drive we were rewarded with an amazing hilltop view and a tiny, lodge-like romantic hotel and restaurant.

First, a romantic dinner, to which Julian responded with a flush of pleasure. He knew where this was going and was already, shall we say, *visibly* in the mood and eating quickly, but I slowed him down. Tonight it wouldn't be about making a baby. It would be about making love. Our love.

I'll spare you the smoldering looks we cast each other during our meal. Suffice to say that when we got to our room I quickly slipped into the chocolate knickers and oy- you should have seen the look on his face when I stepped out of the bathroom dressed only in edible underwear. A look I hadn't seen, let's face it, in a long, long time.

"Is this wonderful sight for me?" he murmured as he pushed me back onto the bed, nibbling on my earlobe and kissing me and... I swear to you in two seconds flat I was a goner. And then... he began to consume his dessert.

I lay back, taking in the magic moment, the way it used to be. Yes, this was Julian, and this was me. And together, we made a wonderful *We*. Forget about baby worries, forget about Maddy mutiny against me, forget about Genie Stacie and her so-called influence on Julian. He loved me. We were a family. And we were on our way back to being like we used to be. Full steam ahead.

Down below, Julian coughed. Then again, making a wheezing sound. I lifted myself up onto my elbows. "What's wrong? Julian...?"

He was turning red and desperately trying to breathe, but nothing was happening. Was he choking on the chocolate? I shot to my feet, beating his back right between the shoulder blades, but it wasn't getting any better. His face was turning purple now as he staggered to his feet, me trying to help him.

Wearing absolutely jack squat, save what was left of my edible underwear, I reached for the phone and dialed an ambulance, threw a tiny towel around myself and flung the door open, shouting for help down the stairs into the darkness of the night.

CHAPTER TWELVE: Underwear and Understatements

Luckily the hotel had been near the *Guardia Medica*.

"Is he allergic to cortisone?" the doctor prompted, his needle poised, ready to inject into Julian's vein something that would either save him or give him the *coup de grace*, or as they say here, *colpo di grazia*.

As Julian's thrashing continued I tried to remember, my mind mush.

"*Signora! Sì o no?*" the demanded, his voice belying the rising panic that a doctor should never show as my mind raced searched for any memories of other allergies.

Oranges, peanuts, cabbages? Yes, yes and yes. But cortisone? I couldn't remember. He was allergic to some kind of drug- I always remembered it, but now, with Julian gasping and the doctor screaming at me I couldn't think clearly.

Was it cortisone...or something that sounded similar?

"*Signora!*"

And then I had it.

"Cardizem! He's allergic to Cardizem!" I cried and the doctor's needle immediately sank into Julian's vein. In a few seconds he was whisked away and I was left behind the swinging doors, propped up against a wall where I took deep, calming breaths. He'd be okay. He had to. I couldn't lose him. And my edible underwear couldn't be the cause of his demise.

When he opened his eyes Julian found himself all tubed up and an IV needle stuck into his arm. His hair all sweaty and matted and his face extremely pale now, he was a real mess (said by the woman now wearing a hospital nightie and with traces of chocolate where chocolate can be fun but only for so long). He looked at me over the mask and I took his free hand, trying not to sag with relief.

"You're okay," I said quickly. "Just a little allergy reaction. Nothing to worry about." Ha. Talk about understatements.

He closed his eyes and blinked once. That must have meant *yes*.

"Mm-hm-hm?" he asked, meaning, I guess, *What happened?*

I blushed. "My underwear...?"

He blinked once. He remembered. "I'm so sorry- I thought it was chocolate. But it was actually *Gianduia* hazelnut fudge..."

Made with the best hazelnuts in the whole of the region. And Julian (how could I forget?) was highly allergic to hazelnuts. He'd had an allergic reaction once when he was a kid that had almost cost him his life.

"We'll look back on this one day and laugh?" I said helpfully to Julian as I sat by his side and he blinked twice, coughed and closed his eyes. I stayed with him for a long while, until he was in deep sleep.

Then I went outside to stretch my legs and pace the corridor in the hospital nightgown they'd given me. At the far end, I leaned back against the wall and closed my eyes. I could've lost him. I could've really lost my husband.

With a sinking sensation of stickiness, I turned to look at the wall behind me and gasped at the big brown stain my butt had left on the pristine surface. I frantically tried to rub it off with the palm of my hand, looking around to make sure there were no witnesses to my abstract art piece.

When that didn't work, I brought my bare knee up against it for more pressure. Still nothing. A nurse stopped short, stared at the nutter (me) who looked like she was trying to crawl into the wall, sniffed the air and nodded for me to follow her.

Inside what looked like a linen closet, she gave me a few towels and a new nightie and led me to the bathroom where she nodded knowingly to the sweet underpants under my towel.

"I heard your husband is allergic to chocolate?" she asked.

"*Gianduia* fudge," I answered and she nodded.

"Next time try caramel," she suggested and left me with a grin.

Next time. Like there would ever be a next time. To think that all this time I'd been extremely careful to keep him away from hazelnuts and now I had almost killed him with my underwear.

CHAPTER THIRTEEN: Poisonous Love

With our romantic buzz dissolving like ice-cream cones on a windy day, my only solution was to work on giving him what he (and I) wanted. The Baby. At this point getting pregnant was a must, by hook or by crook. So like every other woman rapidly running out of ideas while nearing the end of her tether, I re-surfed the net in case I'd missed any of the gazillion tricks listed, keeping his allergies in mind. Medieval, magical or mystical, I was going to try them all.

Scrolling down the long list of miracle-workers I found, in case you wanted to get pregnant and didn't know, were leafy greens, raspberry leaves. Raspberry leaves, really? Never saw that one before. Stinging nettles (been there, done that- it doesn't work, BTW). Neither do grapefruit or yams. Ah. An original suggestion- *headstands*.

I hadn't tried a headstand in a gazillion years. Could I still do one? I used to do them against my bedroom door when I was ten, but now? Only one way to find out. Of course I knew they were no help in getting pregnant. Sperm knew its way around, obviously- but I didn't want to leave any stones unturned. And after a night of horror spent in a hospital, waiting to see if Julian would pull through or die and curse me forever from his grave, can you blame me?

So I closed my bedroom door and cleared the space around it. Then I took a deep breath and bent forward against the door so my hands were adjacent to it. Then I pushed my weight forward as if doing a summersault. The door would stop my legs. All I had to do was let my legs follow my body and keep them straight up against the door.

Staying in that position while Julian… just the thought made me giggle as I leaned forward and, caught unaware, I collapsed in a pretzel shape against the door.

Untangling myself, I peeled myself off the floor and dusted myself off. A fertility miracle-worker or not, I wasn't budging from here until I managed a handstand. How could I not be able to do this anymore? Had I gained that much weight? Lost that much strength in my arms? What, with all my dough-kneading? How had that happened, and more importantly, *when* had it happened?

Was this how old age screwed you over, all of a sudden? One day you couldn't do a handstand and the next you couldn't procreate and before you knew it your hip snapped and you woke up all alone in an old folks' home?

"Enough of this bullshit," I said out loud and tried again, this time against the opposite wall. I flexed my arms, my shoulders and jumped up and down on the spot like a boxer about to face Mohammed Ali. It was now or never. If this wasn't going to help get me pregnant I might as well cross it off my list.

I leaned forward with my arms and lifted my ass in the air, clenching my teeth, waiting to land in a heap again, but then the back of my calves hit the door and there I was, standing upside down. I'd done it! Yes! Now to see how long I could resist upside down.

"Erica, honey?" Julian called and opened the door to our rom. Good thing I'd moved or I'd be flat on my back now. Not that this position was any more regal. We both froze, his mouth open from what I could see from this angle.

"Look, Julian!" I called proudly "I've still got it!"

Silence, during which I remembered what I was wearing underneath. Practically nothing.

"Yes you have," he said with a sexy grin (I didn't see it but I heard it in his voice). "And no signs of fudge anywhere."

I thought I might try and stand up gracefully, but there was no gracefully with having to bend over like that. So I maintained my position, my arms straining, aching, but it was nothing compared to what shape my pride was in.

To make it worse, Julian sauntered over and leaned on the wall next to me. "Need a hand?" he asked gruffly.

"Haha, very good," I answered, trying to ignore the huskiness of his voice.

He watched me in silence and even with my head upside down, I could *feel* the room charge with erotic electricity.

"What are you doing?" I asked, trying to hide the embarrassment in my voice with annoyance.

"Enjoying the view. Nice toenail polish, by the way."

Argh. I was starting to weigh a ton on my wimpy arms. I couldn't hold out any longer, only my pride keeping me in this humiliating position. "Thanks."

"Sure you don't need help?" he asked.

"No thanks. I'm... trying to break a record."

He laughed. "And there was me thinking you were trying to break a leg."

"Stop being obnoxious. It's so typical of you to take advantage," I shot up a him, but I couldn't see him anymore. He'd moved away.

"No," he whispered. "Taking advantage would be doing this." And with that, he placed his hands on my ankles and pulled them slightly apart. I loved a man with a filthy mind.

CHAPTER FOURTEEN: Facing the Facts

Three weeks later, Julian was once again returning from the US, tooting his car as he pulled up the drive.

I breathed deeply to calm my nerves. It wasn't fair to keep yet another IVF failure from him. He was expecting good news, the poor guy.

I delayed it by kissing him at length, and he responded with the usual fervor, his hand cupping the back of my head while he took my mouth in an ah-mazing kiss which told me he'd missed me. So far, so good.

"So tell me, what did she want now?" God, you'd think I'd be able to wait until we got into the house.

Julian sighed and flung his arm around me as we climbed up the steps. I took the hand on my shoulder and kissed it. God, I'd missed him too.

"Genie Stacie did this amateur porn flick years ago and now this guy's threatening to go public with it," Julian said as I dragged him to the privacy of our bedroom to tell him about IVF. Somehow the two conversations didn't seem to fit together so I let him talk about her. If I hadn't been so despondent about my period I would've appreciated the trivia.

So *that* was her secret? But what did it have to do with Julian? Ohmygod! I caught my breath. "Did you star in it, too?"

Julian cocked his head and looked at me. "Do I look like the kind of guy you'd want to see in a porn flick?"

Uh, ye-ah? "Of course not," I lied. "Well, then? How is it your problem?"

Julian shrugged. "Her agent says she should let it go public. It would give her notoriety a boost."

"I'll say. That would let people get to know her for who she really is."

"Erica…"

"What? She stars in a porn movie, for Christ's sake, and you're still defending her?"

"Erica, she was very young, she didn't know what she was doing. And in any case she's a producer now. She's reading some scripts, one of which mine."

She could read? Some people never ceased to surprise me. "But how is this of any interest to you?"

He didn't even need to think about it. "Genie has never had any friends, she's never trusted anyone."

"Except you," I corrected, feeling my hairy eyeball get into gear. I could never stop it. It just went up of its own free will. Julian noticed it and pulled me closer to him.

"Come here, you," he said softly as he always did at the end of the day, and I buried myself in the nook between his arm and his side.

"Genie and I had one thing in common. We were both orphans."

I suffocated the snort and the retort that had flared up naturally. Eight years in idyllic Tuscany and I still hadn't managed to mellow. I really *was* a lost cause. "Ok," I said to fill the expectant silence before he told me her sad story of abandonment and probably teenage prostitution, judging by the look of her, but I kept that to myself. For now.

"We only dated for a short while, that's true, but she opened up immediately, (I suppressed the urge to snort again) and I saw her soft side (was he doing it on purpose now, or are men just born dumb?) because she was very lonely in her environment."

Oh, come *on*! "She doesn't look lonely to me."

"Oh, she is, trust me. All the women were jealous of her career and all the men just wanted to get her in the sack."

"You included," I said, relieved he couldn't see my eyebrow that had lost itself in my hairline somewhere, like a natural face-lift. No wonder I didn't have any wrinkles. I was too sarcastic to let my face stagnate.

"Including me, yes. I was attracted to her-"
"Long legs?"

He chuckled, and drew me closer. "I was going to say fragility, but yes, her looks weren't exactly an obstacle."

"How gentlemanly you are," I said, more sweetly, thus more sarcastically than I'd intended. Man, was I jealous or worse?

One thing for sure, this was going nowhere good. Genie Stacie had found her way into our lives and didn't look like she was going to forget our address any time soon. I wondered how much longer I could put up with this situation. Just knowing she existed was bad enough, but then she started calling his *cell phone*. And that's when I recognized her telephone manners from before, when she'd called me in the middle of the night. I should've remembered her squealing voice. She had already had his cell phone number. She must have called him after she hung up with me. And Julian had never mentioned it. Why, if he wasn't hiding anything?

Why feign surprise when she called to say she was dropping by for a visit? For my benefit? Was something going on and I was totally in the dark?

You might think I'm paranoid, but *you* try discovering that your first husband, whom you thought was working until late almost every night, actually *got off*, and you'll pardon me the pun, precisely at four thirty every afternoon to drive his secretary.

The very secretary who was expecting his baby and living in a beautiful condominium *you* had actually paid for. I knew you'd see where I was coming from, insecure or not.

So now my main questions were:

Number One: Does my husband still love me?

Number Two: Does Genie Stacie represent a threat or not?

Number Three: If so, am I going to murder her?

Number Four: And after I've murdered her? (Go to Question Number One again.)

In record time I'd managed to twist myself into such a knot I was a live wire threatening to electrocute anyone who had enough guts to come anywhere near me. And on top of everything else, no, *more* than anything else, I hated the way Julian treated her. Like he *cherished* her. *Genie Stacie's an orphan, Genie Stacie never had any friends, Genie Stacie is fragile, Genie Stacie needs me.*

And *I* needed Genie Stacie to disappear.

Did Julian feel validated by Genie Stacie's attention? Was I neglecting him? Was that what all this was about, and now it was too late to get my husband back? Had I let him fall out of love with me?

Julian took my hand and I thought he was going to sit me down at the table for a lecture Erica-style, but instead he took the tea towel off my shoulder and led me through the large living room and up to our bedroom terrace.

"Look around you, sweetie," he whispered, and I did.

From the top of our hill I could see the endless patchwork quilt of acres and acres of green, yellow and brown land, our vineyards, the green wheat undulating in the fields, the symmetrical lines on the farmland where Julian had run his tractor, the paddock with his horses, and the large swimming pool- exactly like in the glossy real estate magazines. And it was all ours.

So why couldn't I be happy?

"Isn't this what you've always wanted?" he whispered softly as he pulled me back against him, and I breathed in the fresh cool morning air on my face, his warm chest against my back, and I instantly remembered the hours I'd spent in Boston secretly trawling the internet for a home I could afford, knowing that as long as I remained married to Ira it would never happen anyway- even if I'd won the lottery or found a bargain. Ira had not shared my dreams. Julian did. So what else could I possibly want?

Was it true that when women finally got what they wanted, they began to question the validity of their attained aspirations soon after?

"Is it also what *you* wanted?" I asked, closing my eyes, the landscape I knew by heart imprinted in my mind.

"Of course," he said, after a slight hesitation. Or was I imagining it?

"Really? You're not just saying that?"

"Why would I? You didn't drag me here. I was happy to come."

I turned in his arms and faced him, once and for all. "And are you still happy now?" *Even if you're tempted to sleep with Genie Stacie?* I wanted to add, but didn't dare ruin the idyllic, Tuscan moment.

Julian grinned, and I could see the slightest wrinkles at the edge of his eyes, just above his cheekbones. He put his nose against mine, the way he always did, and we were eyes against eyes. I could see the gold flecks inside his blue irises, just before the aquamarine green outer rim started.

Julian was, yes, a drop dead gorgeous man who should have stayed in his high-flying milieu of sports stars among his models and endorsements. But here he was, instead, with me, with the kids, his writing, our everyday routine, mucking around in the stalls, galaxies away from his previous life.

"As long as you and I are like this, I'm happy," he whispered against my mouth, and I wondered whether the toothpaste still held its freshness in my mouth before I decided it didn't really matter and kissed him deep and hard.

He groaned against my mouth, instantly aroused (heh heh) as I pushed my breasts up against him, thankful I was wearing a good bra that morning.

"Ooh, you're in big trouble now," he murmured as he pulled my legs around his waist and peeled off his shirt, right on our private terrace.

I leaned back and admired his ripped body, running my hands up his arms as he kissed the side of my throat which he knew was my Immediate Ignition Button. Sex on the balcony? Decadent. Yummy.

And then the house phone rang.

I sighed and peeled myself away from him and over to the phone just inside the entrance, already knowing who it was.

"Hi Erica, is Julian there? I tried his cell phone but it's off."

Damn right it was.

"Yep, just a second," I said and stonily passed him the phone and headed for the shower, locking the door behind me.

CHAPTER FIFTEEN: Jealousy

It was a damned good thing I had A Taste of Tuscany to keep me from going insane. And that some of our guests gave me something else to think of. We had the oddest people.

There was one family that never left the house except to swim in the pool. No day trips, no dinners out, not even take-away pizza. And when they did surface, the mother always wore a kaftan that reached down to her feet, as if she was about to step into an imaginary jungle.

But that's nothing. You should've seen the Sweeneys, or, as we still call them today, The Swines. Man, you've never seen such garbage.

At first, we thought they'd be okay people. You know, the average British family with three kids, all in school.

The wife, Amanda, was a downright snob who looked me up and down and kept to herself. A real piece of work. The husband was more of a clown, but all in all, your average family.

Or so we'd thought. They left in the middle of the night (we wondered why as the bill had already been settled) and found the keys hanging on the front gate of the property for just anybody to snatch and help themselves to most of the furniture in that particular wing of the villa. Ah. Did I say furniture? Glad I remembered. When we got inside, the bloody bureau was missing! It hadn't cost much, just a really nice piece I'd bought at the Sunday antiques market, but... what the heck would a family flying to London Gatwick do with a *bureau* on their shoulders?

And then my clever clever hubby put the pieces together. The bureau was in the room with the bunk bed. Too lazy to use the built-in ladder, they got into a habit of climbing atop the bureau for a boost. If I remember correctly, the boy sleeping on the top was a chunky thing. He must've, according to Julian, broken it, and rather than pay for the damages from the deposit, they (I can see the dad, particularly) must have decided to hide the evidence and throw it into some skip on the way to the airport.

But that's nothing compared to what we found inside.

"Jesus. You're going to have a kitten," Julian said as I stepped into the renovated tobacco tower.

I stepped into the front room and, I swear, I felt faint. It wasn't just the smell. It was the seven family-sized *garbage* bags, *open* and tipped over (in their haste to escape, one assumes) and strewn across the floor. Including, for everyone's joy, coffee filters, and something that looked like the remains of a chicken curry.

But the joy didn't end there. The kitchen sink was full of scraps of food (I did tell them we didn't have a built-in incinerator) and tea towels stained with everything from tomato sauce to... wine.

I had to stare at the towels for a few minutes before I even recognized which ones they were, for all the patterns had been blotted out by filth.

Shall we move on into the bathroom? Damp towels in the shower, in the sink, under the sink, dirty underwear and more garbage bags.

So we decided on the spot that enough was enough. We were going exclusive, elitist and affluent. No more families with six kids swinging from the chandeliers and crawling up the walls.

And soon, thanks to Julian's connections, we became the secret haven for the jet-set, stars who needed extreme privacy, like the lovely (and sweet even to my eyes) Eva Sanchez, an Argentinian tennis star/ sex symbol of the moment and former squeeze of Julian, albeit for a month.

She was seeing someone but was afraid he was cheating on her (familiar territory for me) so we'd often have a chat and she'd let me read his text messages and ask me what I thought. The guy was nuts about her. Who wouldn't be? Eva was so down to earth, A real woman despite her fame. Luckily, stars weren't all like Genie Stacie.

"Why did you leave her?" I asked Julian.

He looked at me in alarm, like I was going to start one of my interrogations, but then shrugged. "Some people are meant to be just friends. Eva's a great gal."

"Absolutely, I love her," I agreed.

Trouble was that, I couldn't understand, still living outside of the Beautiful People Alliance, why two gorgeous and nice people who'd slept together and decided to see more of each other, could let the relationship die. I mean, if the sex (cringe of jealousy) was great and conversation was brilliant, what could possibly go wrong in a relationship?

"Only you could ask a question like that," Julian said with a chuckle. "When will you stop thinking it's just about two bodies?"

"Huh? It's not?"

He caressed my cheek with his index, his eyes shining. "Of course not. It's about communion. The kind that lasts beyond everything else. *Our* kind of communion, Erica."

Communion? Sure, we got along great, but what made him not look elsewhere when we didn't? Even you would wonder at it. I mean, he had plenty of choices, if our guests and his army of ex flames visiting were anything to go by.

Starting with Polly Parker, a tap dancer who'd participated in Strictly Come Dancing and had won. (By the way, did I mention Julian was getting all sorts of invites to participate in American and British talk shows, from *Good Morning, America* to *Richard and Judy*? Julian appreciated the attention and had scheduled for a few, but drew the line at anything he couldn't wear his own clothes to.)

Next in the line of his ex loves came Moira Mahoney, owner of at least a dozen fashion magazines and still 'very fond' of my husband. "Hang onto him, Erica," she'd warned me with a wink. And so I do my best.

*

"I have to go to the States again next week," Julian said out of the blue the next day.

What the hell, you just got back, I wanted to say. I was just getting back into the swing of things. Why couldn't he just stay put for a bit and be a husband? And then it hit me.

Was I becoming like Ira, resenting Julian's constant career-travelling? And had Julian become me, looking for ways to stay away?

But unlike Ira, I had a real reason to be pissed off. Genie Stacie. She was, no matter what anybody said, what scared me to death. If she could attract him once, she could do it again. And I didn't want him to go where she would have easy access to him, it was that simple.

How to make him understand without losing my rag?
"New York again?"
"No, San Francisco."

Right into her den. "Oh."

"Why, what's wrong?"

I shrugged. "Well, you just got a call from Genie Stacie and you're suddenly off to The States again tomorrow morning."

As if he had his own private seat on the plane. He probably did.

"Sweetheart, please don't be like that. I got a call from Terry right after that."

I snorted. "Yeah, right." Despite his constant reassuring me, was the old flame between them rekindling again? After all these years of distance, did he suddenly realize that he missed his life in the US and all the models, and that, above all, he missed one particular US model?

He moved away from me. "You know, I'm getting really, really tired of your attitude, Erica. You're judgmental and caustic at the best of times. "What the hell is happening to you?"

I stopped, his words sinking in, cutting like shards of glass. I was very thin-skinned lately and it seemed nothing was going right. I didn't like who I was at the moment, and it was going to have to change. I swallowed back the tears.

"Julian, I'm so sorry… it's just- it's just that I got a call from the doctor- the IVF didn't take…" I finally confessed in a whisper as the tears came.

He swung around, took me in his arms and kissed my cheek, his face solemn. "I'm sorry, sweetie..."

"Yeah... I've been trying to tell you for days but didn't have the courage."

"Silly. It's not your fault. Shall we give it another try?"

My eyes swung to his gratefully and I nodded.

He smiled. "Get an appointment for before I go."

And so on Monday morning after a quick 'deposit' at the fertility clinic I double-parked outside the airport and turned to him bravely. With new hopes for a baby and Genie Stacie calling at all hours gnawing at my last shreds of security and Maddy's constant ignoring me, I felt like life's biggest loser. How much longer could I hold out?

"I hate to leave you now of all moments," Julian whispered, his fingers playing with the strings on my hoodie (I was hitting the gym every day now).

"Yeah, I don't want you to go either, but it's important to pursue your dreams, Julian." *If the outcome depends on you,* I mentally added. Getting pregnant was out of my control. This part, the waiting, was the worst and deep down, I really needed him there with me. But I had to put on a brave face.

"Go. I'll keep you posted."

And so Julian hefted his bag (the one permanently packed in the corner of his office containing his passport, American driver's license, a toothbrush, toothpaste, a few changes of boxers and undershirts and socks, legal copyright documents and a copy of his latest novel but absolutely no condoms). I know because I had a (shhh) snoop in there one morning while he was out in the barn with his horses.

"I'll call you the minute I land," Julian promised, planting a kiss on my lips. But his right leg was already out of the car. He couldn't wait to go. That was the truth.

I pulled him back and he turned in surprise as I kissed him hard, almost hurting my own mouth. "Come back home to your woman soon, Fox." *Validation. Letting him know how much you love him.*

Julian's lips turned into a smile which he planted against my lips again, returning my kiss like he hadn't in a long time.

"Hey, I'll be back before you know it," he said, drying my tears with his lips and nudging my nose as he used to.

I nodded, hanging on to the front of his shirt like a wet blanket, feeling ridiculous about even thinking that he was going to cheat on me and maybe even fall in love with Genie. If he hadn't when he was single he wasn't going to now, right? I mean, now that he had me?

Back then he had all the women he wanted. But now he had *only* me. Was that the problem then? Had he changed his mind? Had he finally wised up about his looks and potential and decided he could do way better than me? Was that what all this was about? I hated myself for even *thinking* it. No intelligent, self-confident woman thinks like that- only spineless losers did.

"Sweetie..."

I looked up and smiled. I must have been a mess. I'd started wearing make-up again (which Maddy didn't even notice because she pretty much avoided me like the plague) and could feel my mascara running down my face. So much for glamour. No wonder he preferred Genie and her Brazilian butt.

"Just go, okay? I don't want you to miss your plane."

"Ok, sweetie. I'll call you when I land."

I nodded and finally managed to smile. Of course he wasn't going to meet up with Genie Stacie. Just because it was her city didn't mean-

"Come on, Julian, we're going to miss our flight!" came an unpleasant squeal and my blood froze. Wide-eyed, Julian turned and saw her as she stuck her head in through the car window.

"Erica, let go of him already, he has to get a move on," she giggled as she opened the door and literally dragged him out.

"I didn't even know she was in the country, I swear," he whispered. And with one last air-smooch, his lean figure sauntered towards the entrance doors that slid open, Genie Stacie linking an arm through his and turning back to wave at me.

I inserted the first gear and took the highway home, my stomach in shreds, and wondering how long she had been in Tuscany, how was it that she hadn't dropped in on us and, most important, how she knew he was taking that precise flight on that precise day.

I also conjured up all sorts of scenarios of them having dinner, then a few drinks up in his room. She'd use all her charm to get him back, or at least to get him in the sack. Because Genie Stacie thought that sex was the be-all and end-all of it. I pictured Julian as he resisted, once, twice, three times, even. Then shrug his shoulders and think what I didn't know wouldn't hurt me.

He would shed his clothes, all the clothes I'd lovingly washed and ironed for him, to stand naked, in all his splendor, in front of her. He'd take her in his arms and lift her onto the bed and… I closed my eyes tight and shoved the idea out of my head. My cheeks were wet.

CHAPTER SIXTEEN: Stefania and Melania

The morning of Julian's return, dreading the IVF results, I whirl-winded my way through the house, cleaning, scrubbing, doing laundry. When I was done, I knocked on Maddy's door, desperate for something more to do.

Now usually she had music on full blast, dancing her little heart away with her BFF Angelica. But this time I found her sitting with Warren on the bed, both sets of eyes downcast.

My own instinctively dropped to the small object in her hands. A pregnancy test. I clung to my laundry basket as if it could keep me from swooning.

"What are you doing with that?" I finally croaked, my voice barely audible, my lungs barely working. Maddy? Impossible. I always knew her every move. She was a little crazy but she wasn't stupid. She would never do anything like that. "Are you...?" I couldn't even pronounce the word anywhere near my daughter's face.

Maddy stared at me as if I'd grown another eye in the middle of my forehead. "Me? Are you crazy?"

My eyes swung back to the packet of the pregnancy test. "Then who is? Someone I know? A friend of yours?"

And that was when the door to her bathroom opened and she emerged, pale and drawn, her eyes huge, like a lost child's.

Friggin', bloody *Stefania*.

*

"Can you bloody believe it?" I shrieked, a moment from pulling my hair out of my scalp. "My stupid stupid son got her *pregnant!*"

Julian's hands came down around my shoulders and I flung them off as if they'd had spikes in them. He hadn't been home an hour from his glitzy sojourn into his jet-set life and already he was plunged back into the not-so-glamorous dramas of domesticity

"What the hell is wrong with these kids? They act like they know everything and they can't even manage to put on a condom? What the hell!"

"Calm down just a bit," he coaxed good-naturedly, his hands back on my shoulders. That was Julian for you. Nothing was ever that bad, that dramatic. He always had a justification for the hiccups in life. "They're just kids."

"Very stupid kids."

He groaned. "For Christ's sake, Erica- stop being so judgmental."

"Judgmental?" I repeated. "That is my- our son! Who's going to have a kid! I'm furious, and scared to death, not judgmental!"

He stuffed his hands into his pockets and huffed.

"People make mistakes, Erica. You can't jump onto their backs every time someone falls out of line."

"A mistake? Gluey ravioli is a mistake- burnt bolognaise sauce is a mistake- but this? This…" I buried my head into my hands and sobbed. Really went for it.

"Sweetie," he whispered. "I know you're scared and angry and hurt. But Warren is all that, too. Tenfold. Trust me."

I sighed, wanting to let go and get angry all over again, but forced myself not to because every time that happened, I felt that big demolition ball swinging in my chest like in the old days. To which I didn't want to go back. But still being an in-your-face American at heart, it was difficult for me to live and let live. This was my family we were talking about here. What was the matter with everybody?

"Sweetie, tell me the truth- is this only about Stefania getting pregnant or maybe just a bit about you not getting pregnant?" he asked softly.

"Oh, that is such a crass crass *crass* thing to say!" I flung at him, but couldn't help wonder how much of it was a lie.

Warren knocked on our bedroom door and poked his head in, his face ashen. The last time I had seen that look on his face was when he had been eleven and in trouble for punching a kid at school.

"Come in, son, we'll work this out together," Julian beckoned him in.

Warren stuffed his hands into his pockets and sat down at the writing desk where I paid our bills. Boy, this certainly was the biggest bill ever- my sons freedom and youth. When you had kids you never knew what was around the corner. But this one was easy- around the corner lurked Melania, Stefania's greedy mother.

*

I saw her through the crack in the door. She sat haughtily, straightening her fake Chanel dress, her bangles clanging with the brisk movements. On her face was the look of greed. From what I could tell, this was only the beginning of it.

"How's she looking?" Julian whispered.

"Still like mutton dressed as lamb," I whispered back, calmer now that I'd had a heart to heart with my son and assured him we would be behind him all the way to hell and back.

Julian nudged me forward. "Come on, let's get this over with once and for all."

"Obviously Warren will marry her and support her," Melania began once we were all seated in the living room, at a safe distance from each other.

Julian, the ever-calm gentleman, held my hand, mainly, I think, to stop me from going for the bitch's jugular. A mild squeeze of his hand and I stopped seeing red.

"Warren is twenty years old and a Medical student," I said pleasantly. "He hasn't got a Eurocent to his name."

At that Melania's eyeballs popped out of her head and I thought I'd have to catch them in mid-air.

"You lie!" she shot back, spreading a hand across the room. You have a big house- a good business!"

"My husband and I have a big house and a good business, yes," I agreed sweetly, unwilling to take her bait. "And we work very hard at it. If Warren abandons his studies to support a family, he will have to go out into the world and earn his own fortune."

But Melania's mind was way ahead of me. Actually, it had rushed all the way to my deathbed. "But you have to leave it to someone when you die!" she cried in panic, realizing she'd hit a hard spot and that her usual pushiness wasn't going to get her very far.

"Eventually, yes. But we're hoping to live a very long life, Melania."

"But you have to give them *something* now that she's pregnant!" she insisted.

"*If,* she's pregnant," I countered with that painful grin still plastered onto my face. "And *if* it's my son's."

She opened her mouth to say something but I raised my voice like Marcy would have at a saleslady in Macy's rudely walking away from her: "Then and *only* then we will discuss the matter again- and the options open to them."

"Options?" Melania repeated dumbly. Then it dawned on her. "Who do you think you are, Mrs. Foxham? This is a Catholic country! We don't go around killing babies like mosquitoes!"

"No?" I said, my eyebrow rising. I knew for a fact that Melania had had several terminations in the last few years. Yes, it's a small town and people talk.

"Mamma…" Stefania said, realizing they were getting nowhere.

"*Zitta!*" she hissed at her daughter to be quiet.

"Warren- say something!" Stefania urged, giving him a pinch in the side. I felt him wince in pain and turned to him.

"That, my son, is just a teensy-weensy preview of what's going to happen if you shack up with these two ladies."

"How dare you talk to me like that!" Stefania spat at me, then turned back to Warren. "And how dare you let her! What's the matter with you?"

Julian stood up and said, "Warren. You are old enough to know what you want, but too young to ruin your life. Think about it and tell us what you want to do."

"I already know what I want to do, Dad," he said, and cleared his throat. I stared at him, feeling my face go pale. *Oh, God,* I thought. *Please make him see the light. Please don't let him become this girl's slave.*

Warren cleared his throat again and took Stefania's hand. "Stefania and I are going to need five minutes alone, if you don't mind."

To which I thought bitterly, Yeah- that's what got you in this mess in the first place.

Melania nodded and scoffed at me as if to say 'You lose, I win a big beautiful house with swimming pool *and* horses!'

*

They weren't in there for more than five minutes but it seemed like my life had come and gone. Melania checked her watch so many times and every time she glanced my way she had a smirk on her face. I wanted to smack it off and bounce her head around the terracotta tiles.

Was my son going to sign his own death warrant? Renounce university, his future because he'd knocked up the girl who would do everything in her power to turn him into her doormat? Years and years of my sacrifices flashed by me, from ferrying him back and forth to soccer practice, baseball, Italian lessons, summer camp- everything I'd done to make sure he would one day be a strong, intelligent man in charge of his future. Which was now going down the drain thanks to a white trash girl and her social-climbing mom.

When the door opened Stefania emerged but I couldn't see her face. As she headed for the door Melania scrambled after her, an expression of sheer terror in her eyes.

Warren closed the door after them and heaved a huge sigh.

"What did you say to her?" I whispered.

He shrugged. "That I had serious doubts it was even mine. There have been some rumors and frankly I believe she's capable of scamming me into marriage. When I asked her for the truth she broke down and told me she was seeing someone else but that her mom had told her to pin it on me because we have money."

Julian slapped him on the back. "Well done, lad," he said, beaming.

"Good for you!" I hurrayed, clapping my hands, relieved my son's brain and backbone weren't on his private parts' payroll and that Melania and I would never be related after all. But, I had to admit, I was sad that Stefania had felt the need to turn to someone that wasn't the father of her child.

It turned out that she was pregnant with Leonardo Cortini's baby. Melania, needless to say, was out of her mind with happiness that she'd struck a much better deal than us. Until, that is, Leonardo brushed them off saying he'd never pay a eurocent to a bastard.

No girl- not even Stefania- deserved to be treated like that. Had Stefania been two years younger the law would have slapped Leonardo into the slammer *senza complimenti,* aka, unceremoniously and gladly. The authorities, I imagined, were looking to catch him out on anything- even littering- just to throw the book at him, like getting Al Capone (or my ex-husband Ira Lowenstein) for tax evasion. People like that had it coming.

As for Warren, he'd acted irresponsibly despite Julian's constant warnings about staying safe (and free). But in the end he'd been mature and wise enough to see through the both of them.

God, I missed the eleven-year-old who'd given Billy Blackmoore eight stitches and peed his bed (to be fair to the fella, that happened after Ira had threatened to kill him).

CHAPTER SEVENTEEN: Agony Aunt

The home phone rang over and over and I let it go to voicemail. It was probably Melania who'd already bounced back with another scheme to wriggle her way into our family.

"Awh, come on, Erica, answer me." I'd recognize that low growl anywhere. Terry, Julian's agent. He was like a grizzly bear, thick-necked and barrel-chested. And as stubborn as a mule. What did he want with me, though?

I picked up. "Terry?"

"I knew you were home. Listen, there's a couple of newspapers that want you to write for them."

"What?" Had he misdialed the number after all? Maybe he was looking for some other Erica, a writer?

"On a regular basis, Erica."

I didn't get it. "You want me to write a weekly column?"

"Not exactly a column. More like a blog. Each week you answer questions sent to an email account we set up for you, and you answer them."

"You want me to be an Agony Aunt?"

"Only without the agony. Be Flippant. Irreverent. Funny."

"Ah. Then it's a dead duck. I don't do funny."

"Of course you do. Julian's told me all about your dry humor."

I wondered what else Julian had told him. Terry had been his agent for quite a while. Did Julian confide in him about our personal life as well?

"Why me, Terry? I'm not a writer."

"No, but you're Julian Foxham's wife."

Ah. Of course. "And I'm supposed to write about being Julian's wife?"

"Julian's still a big celebrity, you know, especially with his last few novels, he's bigger than big."

"So ask him to write the blog, no?"

"No. Women will want to hear from you for guidance. You know, marital problems. You two have a good marriage. Who better to answer their questions?"

Good marriage, I thought with a snort. "Uh, thanks Terry, but no thanks."

"Erica, don't turn this opportunity down."

"Opportunity for what?"

"To tell the world about your opinions. Don't you realize how many people read blogs these days? The media gives you *power*."

"I've no doubt, but what am I going to do with it?"

"Don't say no. I'll call you back at the end of the week. They pay really really well."

And with that the phone clicked and he was gone. I imagined Terry being born with his rough looks and manners, smoking his cigar in his crib. Power. What kind of power could a housewife possibly have from writing a few thoughts down? Really, this guy was unreal.

The phone rang again almost immediately.

"Hello?"

"Erica," Julian breathed from the other side of the ocean. Again. He was spending more and more time away from home that sometimes when he *was* home and say, walked into the kitchen, I would start with surprise.

Terry told me. Are you sure you want to do this?" Now that was annoying. "Why not? You afraid of a bit of competition?"

'Don't be silly, Erica. It's just that Terry can be very persuasive, and I want to make sure you're not being bullied into it."

So he didn't want me to do it? Why? I changed my mind on the spot. I always was a bit antagonistic. I snorted. "Bullied into speaking my mind? Have we met?"

He chuckled. "Ok, have it your way."

"Good. You don't mind if I mention you in my articles, do you?"

"Me?"

"Well, the wife of a celebrity can hardly talk about men without mentioning her own man, can she?"

Julian chuckled. "You're right. Of course I don't mind. Just as long as you keep our private stuff private."

"But I can talk about your career, right?"
"Sure. Are you thinking of promoting my book?"
In a sense, I thought. "Absolutely."

"Well, don't make it too obvious. I don't want to look like my wife is pimping me."

I smiled sweetly s if we were on videochat. "Of course not. You have an agent for that."

"Ok, hun, gotta go. Welcome to my world, luv. Got to go now. Bye!"

And he hung up. End of conversation.

Was that it? No, I'm so proud of you or anything? *Blimey*, as he would say, we had a friggin' parade when he'd decide to start writing again and all I got was a

'Welcome to my world'? Did my accomplishment mean absolutely nothing to him? Maybe he was a talented writer, but I was a housewife with a new career. Well, maybe not a career, but a fun thing to do in the mornings rather than doing the ironing.

Don't misunderstand me here. I'd left a fantastic career in Boston because it was killing me. I wanted to be a housewife and have my own business. And now I had all that.

So answering a few letters every morning was not a career move, it wasn't denying who I wanted to be. I was still a housewife. Only I'd have a little more fun. It wasn't like I was bonking the gardener.

So out of the blue and with absolutely no merit whatsoever, I was hired to answer the questions of poor, unwitting people writing for help on my new bloc called Erica Can Tell U. Boy, at least that part was true- the stories I could tell you. Terry recommended I should be honest and not afraid of speaking my mind. Ha. Some of the questions were light and breezy. Like what was it like to be the wife of a celebrity.

Others brought me straight back to my past, like this one:

Q: Dear Erica,

My husband is not a physically violent man but he is verbally abusive. He'll mutter nasty words under his breath- so only I can hear him- about how fat I've become. This really hurts and I swear I don't recognize the man I married fifteen years ago. Everybody else, including my family, thinks he's a saint. I feel so lonely and hopeless. What should I do?

Signed,

Desperata.

I shook my head and typed.

A: Dear Desperata,

I deeply sympathize with your plight. Marriages are never as easy as they show them on holiday, or real estate commercials. Marriages take a lot of working out the kinks and most probably, in time-

I stopped. In *time*? The poor woman had been putting up with this shit for fifteen years. How long was she expected to go on, smiling and pretending to be an idiot while she was slowly dying inside?

If even for a moment I'd doubted I had anything to say to other women, boy was I wrong. I had no doubts or qualms whatsoever. Besides, it was renowned the blog had a humorous take. I hit Delete and started all over again.

A: "Dear Desperata,

Stab him. Bury him in someone else's garden (but leave an anonymous apology note for digging up their flower bed) and get on with your own life. No one will miss your husband anyway."

There. That ought to do it. Served the bastard right.

*

The day Julian returned I got a phone call from my doctor.

"Dottoressa Bardotti-" (gulp) "-hi."

"I'm sorry, Erica…"

There was no need to add anything. I closed my eyes, envisaging yet another little guy going down the drain. And Julian trying to hide his disappointment. This was the fourth bloody time- how many times would we have to go through this torture to have a baby?

Did we want to book another IVF cycle. "Of course, Doctor," I said sweetly, looking Julian straight in the eye. "Next Monday at nine? We'll be there, thank you."

I hung up and watched Julian's face change as if I'd slowly poured acid all over his lap.

"What? "I prompted.

"Are you sure you want to go through with this?"

"Why not? I'm keeping my promise to you. You said you wanted a baby and I'm gonna give you a baby."

"But this would be our fourth attempt, Erica."

"So? Usually it never works before the fourth."

"So how long do you want to keep trying for?" he asked.

I shrugged, my eyes burning. "Until it works."

Julian stood to his feet and pushed his hand through his hair, looking like Superman staring at a big pile of Kryptonite.

"Wait," I said. "I get the impression you don't want me to try anymore."

"Don't be silly. Of course we can try again. As long as you want to."

I rubbed the back of my neck. "Listen, Julian. I'm doing this because *you* asked me. And now it depends on if *I* want it?"

"I didn't say that."

"You didn't have to," I said, my throat getting dry. "Having another baby was light years away from my mind, remember? It was your idea."

"Meaning you want to stop trying?"

So that was what he was up to, the bastard. He'd changed plans mid-way and didn't know how to tell me. If he got a confession from me it wouldn't be his fault if we never had a baby. I decide to call his bluff.

"No. We'll give it another go." Which sounded like *'Let's see if you're man enough.'*

Silence. He must have thought the same thing. "Right. We'll do that." And then, because he was Julian and not your ordinary man, he scooped me up into his arms and took me upstairs to our bedroom.

*

I breathed a sigh of relief at the sight of Renata's scrawny figure at her gate as she called her dog Argo back. I hadn't seen her in ages, busy as I was writing that damn column now.

"Hi from your neighbor, who's missed you," I scarcely managed as I got off my bike and pushed it past the gate.

"Come inside, it's too hot out here. You must be crazy riding around in this heat."

I shrugged. Only mad dogs and the Foxhams.

"How's your column going? I read it- it's funny."

"Really? It's crazy. People are crazy. But I'm glad to do it."

Writing kept my mind off Genie Stacie's presence in my life, the baby that just wasn't happening, my narrowly-escaped Grandmother-hood and Maddy that was constantly driving me crazy.

And that was only on this side of the ocean. God knew what was going on with my parents- if they were still fighting, if Judy and Steve were okay, how Sandra was taking Vince's infidelity. The list was endless. Even if Julian had told me that I couldn't take the weight of the world on my shoulders, most of the times it felt like I did.

"You've done so much for us, you and Julian. I only wish there was some way I could thank you," she said, taking my hand.

I laughed. "Just please keep looking out for us like you always have."

Renata squeezed my fingers. "I've never stopped, Erica."

*

Q: Dear Erica,

my husband is cruel to me. Whilst I appreciated your heart-felt answer to a previous reader to whom you suggested stabbing, I prefer a more bloodless approach. What do you suggest?

A: Bloodless? The next time he has a bath, throw your hairdryer in the water and close the door behind you. You don't want to be bothered by the look on his face once you've done it, believe me.

Among my Ira-killing fantasies, that one had been my absolute favorite.

*

"You've become a celebrity," Terry said on the phone later that day. He'd got into the habit of calling me often. I wondered why he wasted his time. The Q&A had lots of readers- mainly clueless women who thought they needed direction from someone even more clueless than me. What else did Terry want from me, I wondered. I knew him well. He didn't do nothin' for nothin'.

I instinctively snorted. "Who, me?"

"Are you kidding? You are huge in the States. Everybody loves your politically incorrect approach. You're the best thing since Howard Stern. And there's already a book option for you."

So that was what he wanted. "A book? But I'm not a writer," I protested, feeling the panic rising.

I'd had a hard time completing reports on my staff when I worked at The Farthington. Plus, Julian was the family writer, not me.

"You will be," he assured me. "People like you always have something to say."

"I'll take that as a compliment."

Terry chuckled. "Get back to work. And don't lose track of the most important thing- your blog. Gazillions of women out there are literally waiting for your piece of mind with their morning coffee."

"They are not." Were they?

"Of course they are."

"Well, Terry, to be honest, I wouldn't know. I live in the old world. Maybe I should come out there for a bit, get the feel of things. I've been away for eight years now."

Silence. "Absolutely not, Erica. Your take is original because you *are* out there."

Huh?

"If you came here, you would ruin the mood. You are big here because you're international. Your blog is translated into seventeen languages."

That many? Then how come my finances hadn't changed that much?

So start collecting ideas for your block-buster, writer."

And like in a dream, whenever I sat down to write the story of my youth, my fingers glided across the keyboard as if I was playing some mad symphony I'd invented in my sleep.

I wrote and wrote about my doubts as a mother of a teenage daughter so dangerously full of herself but also so naïve and thin-skinned, tottering over the edge of sex, about my son who had barely escaped teenage fatherhood, technically already a man but who still had the heart of a boy, full of love and wonder for life and girls in general. I wrote about what I knew.

*

Maybe it was his sense of guilt (he knows what for), but Julian concentrated on being positive in view of the imminent IVF results. He was convinced it was going to work this time. So we built our hopes up all weekend together, snuggling up in front of the TV, reading the papers, breakfasting endlessly ("More coffee, sweetie?" "Oh, yes, thank you, and can I have another muffin, please?" "Of course, sweetie,"). Happy. Hopeful. Renewed enthusiasm. At the end of the day we knew that family was the most important thing and if we didn't succeed it was no tragedy. I'd have gained fifty pounds anyway.

The call came at three in the afternoon. I grabbed the phone as if my life depended on it. Because it did.

"Dottoressa Bardotti...?"

"Erica, hello. I'm so sorry. This cycle wasn't successful."

My eyes darted to Julian's face. There was acute hope in it even if he tried to conceal it. He would be gutted now. Me, I was past hoping anymore.

I rang off and turned to him. He took one look at my face and folded me in his arms.

"I'm so sorry," I wept, my arms around him, clutching at his shoulder blades. "It's not working."

"Shh... it's okay, sweetie."

"But it's not ok," I argued. "I know you really want a baby."

The reality finally hit him, and to his credit, he shook his head. "I want you and our family. Anything else is a bonus. Now dry your eyes and let's go for a nice drive. How about a hot air balloon ride?"

"Really?" I said, swiping my eyes. "You're not disappointed?"

"Naw. It'll be fine. Now go and put on your sneakers."

I caressed his cheeks and kissed him. "Don't tell anyone, but you're the best husband a gal could have."

"I know," he said with a grin and turned to look out the window where a cloud of dust was forming on the horizon. A Lamborghini- the same Genie Stacie had rented when she dropped in on us.

Julian and I stared as Genie Stacie jumped out of the car, a younger version of her shyly hanging back.

"Julian, Erica- I'd like you to meet my beautiful daughter Josephine Jackson..."

CHAPTER EIGHTEEN: Joey

"Please-call me Joey," said the young girl offering her hand shyly. Genie and Joey. It somehow sounded like an unfortunate Thelma and Louise spin-off. She was the antithesis of Genie Stacie.

If the word *derelict* had an image it would have been Josephine Jackson's persona. She looked like a little mongrel with her tail between her legs, ready to flee at the first sudden movement. My eyes involuntarily slid to her bony arms. It didn't take a rocket scientist to see she was underfed, just minutes away from starved.

She wore an outfit that was pretty much a copy of her mother's, only she looked very uncomfortable in it, constantly pulling down the hem of her miniskirt.

I loved her on the spot.

"Don't slouch, Josephine," Genie Stacie ordered, her voice like the crack of a whip, and, like a puppet on an invisible string, Joey's back snapped straight, her eyes darting from Julian's to mine. I smiled at her and pulled her into the kitchen where I'd prepared a nice lasagna for dinner. Joey readily held her plate up with a grateful but shy smile.

"No, don't eat that- it's full of grease and calories," Genie Stacie scolded, slapping Josephine's hand and in the process, mine as well. The ladle full of lasagna fell onto my grandmother's precious linen tablecloth and Julian's eyes met mine. I stifled a gasp of mortification. How could a mother treat her kid like that? After years with Marcy I still hadn't learned to gloss over things like that.

As far as the ruined tablecloth was concerned, it served me right. *Never give pearls to pigs*, my grandmother used to say.

"Joey and I are going to Africa next Wednesday," Genie Stacie said as if nothing had happened. I wished she'd go a little further, like maybe the South Pole and stay there until she froze to death.

"Oh?" Julian raised an eyebrow.

"They're finally shooting it, Jules! They're finally shooting Beyond the Dunes!"

Julian's face lit up with genuine pleasure. Only he knew what she was talking about, because it went way past my head. What was so special about the sand dunes?

"It's this project Genie Stacie has been working on for years," Julian explained to me. I made an "Oh," face and nodded as I cleaned up the mess she made. It seemed to me that was all I was doing lately, cleaning up after her, while she ignored me as if were her housekeeper.

"I'm producing it!" she beamed.

"Genie Stacie, that's absolutely brilliant! Congratulations, old girl!"

"Yeah, congrats," I added. "How long are you staying away?"

"Oh, at least six months! Joey is dying to see Africa, aren't you, sweetie?"

Joey, who was busy surreptitiously stuffing her face, blinked at her mother, then at me. And fainted.

"Oh, my God! Joey, wake *up*!" Genie Stacie screamed as Julian bolted out of his seat and scooped the girl up in his arms. He lay her on the sofa and I made a dash for my salts.

"Here, put this under her nose," I said and Julian waved the tiny bottle in front of Joey's face.

"Joey?" I called softly.

She turned her head, opened her wide eyes, yawned and looked straight at me in wonder. It was like watching her being born.

"What happened?" Genie Stacie wanted to know. "Joey, you're not pregnant, are you?"

Julian glanced at me and I rolled my eyes.

"Of course not, Mom," she murmured. "I'm just tired."

As if you needed a degree in Medicine to see that.

I had Julian put Joey in the gold guest bedroom upstairs and stay with her and Genie Stacie lest the idiot do or say something she'd be sorry for.

The banging of my crockery downstairs spoke books on my opinion as I quickly nuked a beef stew I kept for when the kids had colds. Forget chicken soup, in this house we ate heartily. Even Maddy.

Josephine opened her eyes as I tiptoed in and tried a smile. The poor kid looked at the mug with lust as I shooed Julian and Genie out so he could lecture her (he was good at that, while I usually simply attacked) and I could put some nutrients into that poor girl. She must have been at least twenty pounds underweight. How can a mother *not see*?

"Just a little stew," I whispered as she tried to prop herself up. I recognized a faint whiff from my pregnant days.

"Did you vomit, sweetie?" I asked as I patted the pillows down.

She looked up at me miserably and whispered, "It's not like it seems, Mrs. Foxham. I just don't understand."

I swear I had to fight to stop the tears from gushing. Tears of compassion, tears of fury. Tears of fear for this girl trapped in her mother's lifestyle. "I know, Joey. It's only normal. You need to get back to eating gradually."

She nodded and sipped the soup to the very last drop, raising her eyes at me in gratitude, and I wanted to cry all over again.

"Here," I said, slipping her a tiny chocolate.

Her eyes widened. "Oh, I can't," she whispered in horror. "My mom would kill me."

"Does your mom always keep you on a strict diet?"

"I'm on a vegan non-dairy diet," she explained with a wince.

I rolled my eyes.

"It's because I tend to get fat," she added in her mother's defense.

And then, looking down at this young girl in the bed, I knew what to do.

*

"Fat!" I spat later in the bedroom as Julian and I were getting ready for bed. "Can you imagine that? Your friend is a psycho, Julian. A bloody psycho, and someone should lock her up before she kills her daughter!"

But Julian was too indignant to even answer, his jaw tight. "She was always a bit of a flake, but my God, how could she have changed so much?" he said softly.

"Because she is a *nullity*," I sentenced fiercely, feeling the tears coming back. "She doesn't even deserve to be a mother. She has no idea of what it means to take care of someone!"

I swiped at my eyes, then my cheeks and chin as Julian opened his arms for me, but I was too furious to take harbor in them. I began to pace back and forth at the foot of the bed.

"Sweetie, Hollywood is full of anorexic teenagers. Maybe it's not her fault after all. Girls today want to be slim- look at Maddy."

"Don't... compare that ghost of a girl to my daughter."

"*Our* daughter," Julian corrected me softly but firmly.

"Josephine is not anorexic," I informed him. "She downed some stew in three minutes flat, the poor kid."

Julian grinned, then frowned. "She did? That means she's not anorexic, right?"

"Terrified of her mother, that's what she is," I sentenced. "The girl is starving because her mother won't let her eat properly. No meat, no fish, no eggs, no cheese. She's allowed to eat only vegetables, fruit and wheat germ! At eighteen? What the hell is that all about?"

Julian ran his hand through his hair. "You're absolutely right."

"Can you imagine that poor starving girl having to face the next six months in Africa where already the food is so scarce?" It was obvious that I wasn't going to let Genie Stacie take Joey anywhere. "*And* live with someone like Genie Stacie?"

"Well, she is Joey's mother," Julian said half-defensively, and I whirled around on my heels to face him. "That is exactly what is wrong with this world."

"Well, she's got full custody," Julian said. "Tom doesn't even pay her alimony, nor does he care about the kid."

Well, Julian seemed to know pretty much about it. I could already see Genie Stacie pouring her heart out to Julian about how hard it was to be a star and a single mother, and the schmuck listening sympathetically. Puh-lease!

"If a woman can't be a proper mother…"

Julian glanced at me as my voice cracked again. "You okay, sweetie?"

I dashed my knuckles across my eyes and nodded. I was *not* going to take this personally. "In the meantime, other women, good, capable women, are dying to have kids."

"Honey…" he whispered as he wrapped his arms around me.

"I don't mean only me… just… women, you know?" I sniffed, holding him close. *And* men, who've always wanted to be parents but were never blessed. I'm lucky. I have two kids, but good people, people like you- you deserve to experience the joy of being a father…"

He held me in silence for a long moment, until his embrace became stronger, tighter and he bent to kiss my mouth.

"Well, we'd better hop to it, then, love."

I wiped my eyes and grinned. "Now?"

"Hell, yes…" he moaned as he tugged at my clothes and his, leading me to our shower at the same time.

Julian slipped out of his trousers and turned on the hot water. I was watching him without really seeing him.

"I know they have caterers in Africa, but-"

He pulled my dress over my head and expertly unhooked my bra.

"Panties off, luv."

"But who's going to take care of Joey while the *star* is so busy showing her butt off? I mean, look how skinny the kid is."

"The nanny, I guess," he said, tugging at the last item on his list and pulling me under the jets. "Now let's get you nice and soapy…"

"Uh-huh. Julian, I've got another idea. Let's get Joey off her mother and keep her here for the summer." I could put that kid into shape in no time. "What do you think? It would be an act of kindness toward the kid."

"Good old you with the heart of gold," was all he said as he lathered my hair, then my shoulders, bringing his lips down to mine, but I knew I had his approval. He was not impartial to Joey's fragility either, I could tell. There was just one problem.

"Do you think Genie Stacie'll give us a hard time?"

"Only one way to find out," Julian said as continued to kiss me.

"So when are you going to ask her?" I persisted.

"Later," he answered, travelling down to my stomach, but all I could think of was Joey. In my mind's eye she was already putting some flesh on those bones, ditching the skimpy clothing and actually smiling. Just one summer. That was all I needed.

"Julian- let's not waste any time."

"Anything you say baby," he drawled. I stopped him, and he looked up at me, water dripping down between his thick lashes.

"On second thought, I'll do it," I said and Julian sighed as he pushed me back against the tiled walls slippery with steam.

*

"Genie Stacie, can I talk to you for a minute?"

She bristled and planted her sky-blue eyes on me. "About?"

I coughed. "I'd like- Julian and I would like Joey to spend the summer with us. We think she'd be much happier with kids her own age."

Genie didn't bat an eye. She shrugged. "Okay. I'll leave her here then. Just as long as you don't overfeed her while I'm gone." Then she threw a disdainful look at me. "I want her to still have a semblance of a neck when I get back."

A retort rose to my lips but I pushed it back down as Julian entered the kitchen. He hadn't heard a word. Just typical. If I had voiced *my* thoughts you can be sure he would have made his entrance in that precise moment. Why did Genie always come squeaky clean out of everything and I always got stuck in the mud? Because she had style. A loud, fake style, yes, but nonetheless style. She was the princess and I was the peasant-girl.

"I've had enough. I'm going to bed. I'll see you when you get back, Genie."

Tomorrow morning she'd be out of my house and hopefully out of our lives as well. At least for a while.

*

"She's an absolute liar- and a devious one, too!" I vented as I ripped off my clothes. Julian sat on the edge of the bed, watching me, halfway between what I could only hope was interest in my state of undress and dignified stupor at my story.

"I know. She always was. That's one of the reasons we broke up."

"Gee, I can't imagine what the other ones could be," I continued, dragging my hair into a pony tail. "Just how the hell do you put up with her? I personally would like to drag my fingernails across her face. But you already know that, don't you? And the next time she touches you I will."

Julian chuckled. I stopped and pinned him with my hairy eyeball. "You think this is *funny*? I'm on the verge of a nervous breakdown here! I really will kill her if she doesn't stop!"

"She's leaving tomorrow, sweetheart. Then we won't see her for at least six months."

"Amen. I wish it was six years."

*

In two weeks Joey gained weight and got some color into her cheeks. The dark smudges under her eyes were gone and even her skin and hair improved. She had blossomed under our roof. That's what a little love and healthy food will do to you. I should know.

Although Maddy was two years younger, she and Joey became inseparable. She took her to dance classes and out with Angelica and the rest of their friends.

Genie Stacie had never made time for Joey, giving nothing up- not her modeling, nor her acting. Genie Stacie had it all- and was treated like a princess, no matter what she did or didn't do.

"Why do you let her get away with murder? And who's to say you're still not attracted to her? She's gorgeous- even *I* can see that."

Julian sighed again, this time more audibly. "Yes, she is gorgeous. Even more so back then. But I was young- you've got to cut me some slack, Erica. I forgave you your chef." Meaning that little thing that had almost make us go our separate ways a few years ago. He was right. So I decided to gloss over that one.

"I wouldn't normally do this, but for your own peace of mind I have to tell you something."

I pulled on my ponytail, frantically rolo-dexing through the possibilities, and my finger always landed on the same card- the *I've fallen in love with someone else* card.

"Genie has a drink problem," Julian said with a sigh. "She always has. And when she showed up drunk at the party, I knew Hollywood would slam her, so I took her home immediately. And before you even ask, she passed out and I slept in an armchair next to her bed, furious with her for doing this for the umpteenth time, and missing you.

I stared at him blankly, relieved, for now. So Genie was a junkie. What star wasn't? "Is that why you left her?"

"To be exact, she left me. For Tom Jackson."

"Oh." Meaning she had broken his heart and not vice-versa. So it wasn't a sense of guilt that kept him linked to her. It was something else. If he couldn't hate her for dumping him, then what exactly were his feelings for her? That tallied up pretty dangerously for me.

Tom Jackson was still a movie star the caliber of Ewan McGregor, only older, with the charm of Sean Connery. Scotland one, England zero.

"And she needs help. Please don't feel threatened by her."

"Whatever."

"You can't ever tell her that you know," Julian was saying. "She's extremely susceptible and vulnerable and her self-confidence is on the razor's edge."

Here we go again with the crystal-delicate doll attitude, I thought, then giggled despite myself. "You sound like her shrink," I said.

"Erica, it's not funny. Not everyone's like you."

I felt my smile fall. "Not like me? What does that mean exactly? Sane? Because that's just a façade, you know, my all-business kind of manner, Julian. In truth, I have absolutely no idea what I'm doing half the time. So you see, my dear husband, Genie Stacie and I are more similar than you think after all. Minus the Brazilian butt, of course."

I absently scratched at a scab on my knee and blood gushed out as if to symbolize the way I was feeling. I wanted to see blood, but not mine.

"Shit," I swore, and Julian caught a Kleenex and bent down in front of me to wipe up the blood. I watched the top of his beautiful head, wondering how such a gorgeous guy had got lumbered with me. He reached into the drawer and placed a band-aid on my skin, giving it a light pat. "There you are, sweetie. Better?"

I nodded, a strange knot forming in my throat. "Better, thanks."

"What? Why are you looking at me like that for?" he asked.

"I'd have married you even if you had been the hunchback of Notre Dame," I gushed, out of control. No doubt about it- after eight years, I was still under Julian's spell.

*

Although my blog *Erica Cantell-U* was about how to deal with men, I also got the idea for a book about younger women's problems, *Virginity and other*

Albatrosses, my story about an ugly duckling. Hell if I had enough material for it. I had been the ugly duckling all my life, battling year after year to get rid of my albatross. But to think that my own daughter would in a few years be doing the same made me very uncomfortable. I had given it to her to read for some feedback.

"So what do you think about it so far, Madeleine?" I ventured, mostly to get her to talk to me again. Ever since Genie had arrived, our relationship was not good. At this rate we'd become complete strangers.

She shrugged from her bed, eyeing the dresser where my manuscript lay.

"What do you think about Lisa? Should she sleep with Mike?"

"How the hell should I know? I can't relate to her."

Arrgh. Brutal. "Don't you, uhm, think other girls might?"

"Only losers," was her verdict.

"So you can't see any of your friends reading my book?"

Maddy sighed. "I'm not pimping your work for you, Mom."

Wow. When had my only daughter become similar to Ira?

220

"Okay," I said, taking my manuscript off her dresser and striding out the room, my chest hurting.

Down in the kitchen Joey was making herself a sandwich.

It was a joy to see she felt at home and even more of a joy to see her eat without me having to force-feed her.

"Want one?" she asked and I shook my head. While my own kids were killing me with each passing day, I literally fell in love with Joey. Everything she did, everything she said, was cause of the deepest joy to me. Who knew I'd ever appreciate something Genie Stacie had made?

"What's that?" she asked, eyeing the pile of sheets that used to be my masterpiece in progress.

"Just a book I'm writing."

"Wow, really? Can I see it or is it a secret?" Joey asked, putting her sandwich down and wiping her hands carefully, already reading the first page.

"It's a YA, so it's safe. Nothing like Julian's rubbish."

She chuckled and continued to read.

"Wanna read it all and tell me what you think?" I asked.

She looked up at me, sea-green eyes huge. "Really?"

"Absolutely. Take it with you. Let me know."

"Oh, wow, thanks, Erica! I'll give it back tomorrow morning."

"No you won't. I want you to sleep tonight."

"Mom never lets me read in bed."

Of course not. What an absolute twit Genie Stacie was. Would she never cease to surprise me?

Ten minutes later Genie Stacie knocked on my door. "Julian? Are you in there?" she whispered and I opened the door.

"Oh," she said. "I was looking for Julian."

What the hell are you still doing here? I wanted to answer, but instead said, "Try the stables."

"Right- where else would a stallion be?" she quipped.

"I beg your pardon?"

She shrugged. "Nothing you would understand."

I crossed my arms in front of my chest. "Maybe you want to explain it to me."

She chuckled. "Never mind." And as she turned to go, she muttered, "What a waste of hunk."

"I beg your pardon?"

She put her shades on indifferently, as if I hadn't even spoken. "Julian is not interested in you anymore. I'm surprised he ever was."

I stared at her. She hadn't really said that, had she?

"Look at yourself- you're huge, anonymous, you dress like you have no clue and all you do is cook and eat, cook and eat."

"And you? Why don't you go back to your little old bottle and leave us alone?" I said before I could stop myself.

At this point Julian appeared at the bottom of the stairs and looked up at us in shock.

Shit. I'd meant it as a Genie-in-the Bottle pun- not to let on that I knew about her drinking problem. I felt horrible. Julian closed his eyes and raked a hand through his hair.

Genie Stacie's eyes popped out of her head and she looked at Julian in anguish. "You told her!" she squealed as he slowly came up the stairs, his eyes darting to mine, hurt. I'd betrayed his confidence in me. I'd never done anything like that before.

Shit, shit, shit. How the hell was I getting out of this one?

"Told me what?" I asked, desperately thinking of something to undo what I'd done. "Look, I'm sorry about the Genie in the bottle comment, but really, what the hell was your mother thinking when she named you?"

She looked at me, then at Julian as she squared her shoulders and sniffed. "Never mind."

Not knowing what to do or say, I turned and went back inside bedroom, seething and feeling like the world's biggest shit at the same time.

CHAPTER NINETEEN: Fourth and Final Attempt

Genie Stacie finally gone, Joey seemed to relax. The family picture we took during a trip to the beach was sitting on Joey's bedside table. A small knot formed in my throat. Poor thing. There were no other pictures. Not of her dad, not of her mother, not even of herself. Well, that was going to change here and now. So I went out and got her a large frame.

"You can put all your favorite snapshots in here," I said as she unwrapped it and kissed me on the cheek.

"Can I go get my camera then, and take some around the house with you guys?"

The knot in my throat had blocked my air passage, so I just nodded as she skipped off happily, her lanky legs like a colt's, so similar to Maddy.

Denial was a vicious beast. I didn't need Dr. Denholm- or even a two-year-old for that matter- to tell me what I was going through.

In my desperation to become a mother I was willing Joey to need me, willing her to recognize in me a dependable source of affection and stability, love and comfort. In my mind, I'd already moved her in under our roof, enrolled her at our local school, helped her decorate her own pretty room, cooked her reconstituting meals instead of a granola bar for dinner. In my mind she was my daughter and not Genie's.

Sunday was her birthday. I made all her favorite dishes and Maddy, Warren, Julian and I had secretly collected a series of presents in my closet.

"Happy birthday, sweetheart, I chimed as we all sang out of key, and she slapped her forehead and giggled.

We all hugged her and sat on her bed. "What would you like to do today, Joey?"

"I don't mind," she whispered.

"Oh come on, birthday girl! It's your day. Choose anything."

She hesitated, her eyes wide as she looked at me in wonder, kind of like a mixture between love and gratitude. God, what a feeling! "Anything?"

I beamed down at her. "Absolutely."
"Well, I'd love to play baseball."
"Baseball it is!" Warren called, and soon the mob was calling teams. I glanced at Julian who squeezed my hand.

*

"I'm ready for my next treatment," I told Julian as I was dishing lunch up for the two of us. Warren was in Siena for the week for an exam and Maddy was with, you guessed it- Angelica.

He stared at me. "You are?"

God, we weren't doing this again, were we?

He rubbed the back of his neck. "I mean, you're always so busy, flying back and forth to the States for your book and all."

He wrapped his arms around me. "A child is more important than a book. If you're ready to start again, I'll postpone my book tour. No biggie."

Postpone his book tour? His career? How was I going to be sure he wouldn't regret it soon enough?

"No, that's okay. After you make your, uhm , deposit, you can go. I can handle the rest on my own."

"You must be out of your mind if you think I'm going to leave you at a time like this," he said, kissing my forehead, and I wished he'd kissed me on the mouth.

"No, really," I choked. "It won't work anyway, and you'll have lost an opportunity for nothing. Really. Go."

"Don't talk like that," he whispered, rubbing the back of my neck. I closed my eyes, relishing the feel of his hands on me, willing him to go a little lower, down the front. But he didn't, and I realized how sad it would be to have a kid without the two of us even having sex.

"You need to be positive, my girl."

I snorted, trying to keep the sudden tears back. It wasn't working. It was just a waste of money, hopes and time. I hated to see Julian become so hopeful and then deflated. But he sure as hell did a great job hiding it.

Especially now that his book was out and he was whizzing around the world faster than his Supersperm ever could.

"Tell you what," he said. "When we're done at the clinic, why don't we go for a little vacation, just you and me? We'll leave the kids with Caterina, and Renata can look in on them from time to time."

So he already anticipated the consolatory trip? He really pissed me off sometimes.

I sighed and went upstairs to work on my e-column.

Q: Dear Erica,

My husband doesn't want to have a baby because he says all my attention will go to it rather than to him. What can I do?

A: Buy your husband a pacifier and stick him in a playpen and post pictures of him on Facebook. That should do it.

Q: My husband is really good-looking and when we go out, sometimes he walks ahead of me, like he doesn't know me. I sometimes get the feeling he's ashamed of me. What can I do?

A: Don't go out with him. And poison his dinner.

Q: My husband complains my career has supplanted my family time and that he sees our

228

housekeeper more than he sees me. As a matter of fact he's bonking her. What should I do?

A: Hire a cleaning boy and bonk him.

Q: My husband prefers gardening to having sex with me, and now I keep dreaming I'm having sex (one at a time) with all my ex-boyfriends who make me feel beautiful and sexy. What should I do?

A: Let your husband mow the lawn. Call all your ex-boyfriends and have them (one at a time so it lasts longer) mow you.

At the end of my day, and sick and tired of miserable marriages, I knocked on Julian's door. He'd been in there all afternoon and I was getting curious. "Julian? Is ricotta ravioli okay for dinner?"

He was at his desk, head in his hands, his face red, his eyes wet. My gaze darted to his laptop screen but it was still off. Instead, his cell phone was lodged in his fist. "Julian, are you crying? What is it? What happened?"

But he was silent, and slowly lifted his head to look at me and my stomach lurched. Had there been an accident? Was someone ill?

"Julian please, you're scaring me…"

He watched me for a moment, his green eyes drowned in tears. Shit, I'd never seen him this way before. He drew a deep breath.

"Sit down, Erica…"

Here it was- the *talk* I'd dreaded since he told me he loved me eight years ago. He wanted to leave me for greener (or blonder) pastures, and I was weighing him down. He wanted to pursue his career as an author because he believed in it- a career that he couldn't pursue exclusively from an old Tuscan farmhouse. We'd fared pretty well, if you considered that the benchmark for marital crises was normally seven years. I'd cheated fate out of a few months.

My mind shot back to eight years before while, amidst fights with my first husband Ira, I'd squirrel myself away with my laptop and scroll down properties available on all the Tuscan real estate websites. And then my BGFF Paul had found me this property through a friend of his.

Maybe I was getting ahead of myself. Maybe he didn't want to leave me- maybe he wanted me- us- to go with him? Maybe he wanted us to move back to the States? But I dismissed the thought even before it mushroomed, big, black and ugly in my mind. Julian knew exactly how happy we all were here. This was our dream. But, to be fair, it had never been *his* dream.

He was rubbing the back of his neck, the way he always did before facing a problem. Correction- before getting rid of a problem. I squared my shoulders, ignoring the pricks at the back of my eyeballs. This was it. The end of an era.

He whirled around. "Genie Stacie just called."

I closed my eyes and swallowed. Here it came. The end of our marriage.

"She's on her way back from Africa and..." he stopped and took a huge breath, his Adam's apple moving visibly. "...I'm Joey's father."

CHAPTER TWENTY: Family Strangers

"I'll have to take a paternity test, but Joey's birthdate matches the time I was seeing Genie."

Personally, I didn't need any evidence. It was in Joey's face, a lovely female version of Julian's. Joey had Julian's eyes, hair, even his teeth. How had we not seen it before?

I imagined him, years ago, younger and already gorgeous, gallant and available. And a real heart-throb. Who could resist him? Not me. Nor Genie Stacie. One night (or day, the details were irrelevant and his business anyway) of crazy sex had done it, as it usually does- for other women, because I'd tried everything to make a kid at this point.

If Joey really was his daughter, then she was the only person he knew that had his blood, because he'd been adopted. He didn't know where his real parents were, nor if they were still alive.

It kept roiling around and around in my brain, looking for a place to rest and settle.

Julian has a daughter. From another woman.

We'd been trying for months now. And now we could stop because Genie Stacie had come to the rescue.

I couldn't understand why she'd stayed away all these years, but the more I thought about it, the more it made sense. Joey, so sweet and smart, could only be Julian's daughter. And in a sense, I was relieved. Relieved that Julian could have a say in changing that poor girl's life and offer his unconditional love. We could keep her here with us, offer her a normal life.

But on the other hand? We'd moved to Tuscany eight years ago as a family, with a million visions of happiness in our heads- our dream home, our dream businesses, our dream life which we had truly earnt. We deserved to finally be here, together. But if our dreams had come true, they hadn't lasted all that long. Because now we'd never get rid of Genie Stacie. She would always be part of our lives.

Was this was what life had turned out to be, while we were busy dreaming of our perfect future? Another woman from his past, with his child- had this been Fate's plan all along?

Up until now Maddy had been his only daughter, and he'd seemed to be perfectly happy with the arrangement. Yes, I knew Julian wanted a daughter of his own, but I never thought it would be his and someone *else*'s. Where did that leave me? Was I just being selfish, or my usual terrified self? Julian had a right to have kids, but only *my* kids, I'd always thought. But now things were different.

This wasn't about Julian leaving me for another woman and having kids with her. This was about a human being, a child that already existed and that deserved to have a dad. And while we were at it, a real mom, too- not just a bimbo in hot-pink heels.

"Erica, honey? Talk to me…"

I looked up. And took him into my arms. How much did I love this man?

"It's okay," I whispered. "We'll take care of Joey. See if we can convince Genie Stacie to leave her here as much as possible."

"I'm so sorry to do this to you, Erica…"

I caressed his cheek, realizing that things would never be the same.

"…but we will continue to be happy together, no matter what fate throws our way," he whispered.

Happy? Happy? I couldn't remember the last time I'd laughed since Genie Stacie landed on our home. Like a bomb. Like the plague.

Just then Julian filled the distance between us, taking my face in his hands.

I looked up at him and saw my delicious British principal of yesteryear, the one who swore eternal love to me. Had we been happy until then?

*

Even if Julian hadn't confirmed it officially to the world (Terry's advice was a terse *No Comment*) we knew, felt it in our bones that Josephine Jackson was Julian's biological daughter. Someone who finally shared his DNA.

No comment? I wished it had been that easy for me. If I could keep my mouth shut on my feelings of anger. Betrayal. Julian, without wanting to, had betrayed my dreams of happily ever after. Because my ever after wasn't going to be so bright from now on. Even if I loved Joey.

*

"It was just sex, Erica. And it happened years ago," Judy said to me as I crouched in the darkness of the study during my one a.m. rant. "Although of course the bitch could've told him a little sooner."

"Yeah, that's what I keep telling myself," I whispered as a thought hit me.

If Genie Stacie had told Julian she was pregnant years ago, what would Julian have done? Would he have married her? Would they have lived happily ever after? One thing was for sure- he never would've saved me from my Spider Attack in that restaurant nine years ago. The thought scared me. What would my life have been like without him? Would I have found the courage to come out here and live in Tuscany? Or would I have settled down with a colleague at The Farthington in Boston? Genie Stacie, that little schemer, had played a very important part of my life. At the end of the day it was thanks to her dumping him that I'd met Julian. And now thanks to her I would soon lose him.

"What if it wasn't just sex? What if Genie Stacie really had meant more to him? Don't forget she was the one who dumped *him*."

"Yeah, for an older man," Judy said.

"All the same, the damage has been done."

*

So Genie was coming back from Africa to discuss Joey. But she got in sooner than expected and way before Julian. I'd promised him I'd be on my best behavior.

"Have a seat, Genie Stacie, would you like some coffee? Julian won't be back for another hour," I explained as she barged through the kitchen door, sporting a Hermès (I know because it said so in big silver letters) bag the size of a boom-box.

"Why can't you just read the writing on the wall?" she bit off. I stared at her, the coffeepot in mid-air. This wasn't how I'd envisaged our encounter. What writing on the wall was she talking about?

"Julian and I are getting back together again. He doesn't want to have your child. He wants mine. As he did years ago."

He'd *wanted* a baby from her?

"And you even ask yourself why Julian doesn't find you attractive," Genie Stacie said smugly, tsk-tsking and shaking her head.

I looked up at her. Surely my hearing was playing tricks on me? "I beg your pardon?"

"Look at yourself, Erica. You wear track suits for Christ's sake!"

"Just around the house…"

"Yeah, and I've seen how often *you* leave this mausoleum."

I stood up. "Ok, Genie, I think I've had enough. You have absolutely no right to come to my home where my children and my husband- the operative word being *my*, live in total happiness."

"Total happiness?" she echoed, snarling, her face so not pretty now. "He's *done* with you. Everyone can see it but yourself. So stop writing those pathetic columns about relationships because you don't have a clue about how to keep your *own* man," she added before she turned on her heels, leaving her leather boom-box on the kitchen table and me still holding the coffeepot like a moron.

Now with Genie Stacie it had become an open, all-out war. She had openly declared her role of husband-snatcher.

"Mom?" Maddy called me from the front door.

"Yeah?" I called back, my heart still pounding even after Genie had marched out of the room a full ten minutes ago.

"I'm going out with Genie Stacie, Angelica and Joey, okay?" So she was talking to me after all.

"Go right ahead!" I figured she was better off not seeing me so miserable. Genie Stacie's own daughter wasn't enough. Let her move in on my own, too.

I ditched the coffee and poured myself a glass of wine instead, sinking down into the sofa. As much as I hated to admit it, Genie Stacie was right- I always wore track suits or jeans. Or even my PJs when we didn't have guests. I *was* a mess.

I poured myself another glass of wine, thinking I shouldn't be drinking on an empty stomach so I made myself some popcorn. There was a Queen special on MTV so I sat and watched as Freddie Mercury pranced around the stage, his melodic voice coming out of the speakers, filling the room with a tangible warmth and sense of sadness. Love Of My Life, he was singing, and I grabbed another handful of popcorn and jammed it down my throat to stop the tears from surfacing.

Julian *was* the love of my life- the only man in the world I could ever love.

Before I knew it, I was reaching for my third bottle, swaying now to the notes of Bohemian Rhapsody, the part where it becomes pure, angry rock.

Man, I loved this song! *"So you think you can love me and leave me to die-ie!"*

"Erica?"

I whirled around with my glass, spilling red wine- *shit*- all over the white rug. Julian. He took a closer look at me. "Are you... *drunk*?"

"Of *courshe* not," I answered. "I'm just shinging wit' Freddie."

But Julian took the remote and Freddie disappeared from the screen. I groaned. Julian sighed and sat down, patting the sofa next to me. "We need to talk, sweetheart."

"I don't want to talk. I want to shing!"

Julian groaned. "You're absolutely sloshedHow long has this been going on?"

"You'd know if you were around," I snapped. Boy, could I smell a bruiser of a fight coming. One that would've sobered anybody.

He gently took my wrists and sat me down on the sofa next to him.

"Listen," he said, softly but so firmly I focused my attention on him as if he was delivering some important speech. "I know how freaked you are because it's the same for me."

I snorted and he put his finger under my chin so I had no choice but to really focus. Boy, was it hard, with the wine and the rhythm of the music still swaying and swirling inside my mind. But I tried all the same.

"Has this ever happened before?" he asked. "Have you ever drunk this much?"

With images of Marcy's drunken and embarrassing moments of truth, I sobered instantly. "No," I said. "I swear. This is the first time."

Luckily Julian believed me. His face cleared instantly. "Good. Because you are my rock, Erica. Ad I can't see you crumble. Especially when I need you so much."

"You need me?"

His eyes swept over my face.

"More than ever."

"Oh, I need you too, Julian," I groaned, wrapping my arms around his neck and he hugged me tight, so tight I thought he was going to break me. I rained little kisses on his neck and ear, running my fingers through his hair, over and over again, until he pulled away to look me in the face. His own eyes were hooded now, and I could feel the unmistakable, rock-hard bulge that meant not only he had forgiven me, but that he'd forgive me anything. But then I suddenly remembered.

"Oh, no- we can't. They'll be back soon, Genie Stacie and the girls."

"She's already here?"

"We had a bit of a run-in."

Julian groaned. "Erica-"

"It was her fault this time, I swear it. She told me the two of you were getting back together again because you wanted her babies and not mine. Or something like that, I can't remember. And then she took my baby shopping. Or whatever, I don't know. It hurts to think. In any case, she was awfully convincing about you and her."

Julian looked at me at length, and then poured me a nice hot cup of coffee and drew me into his arms. "You know that's absolute shite, don't you?"

"Uh... uh-huh?" I asked, looking up into his sexy, take-me-now eyes.

"Uh-huh," he confirmed, a big grin on his lips. "Now let's go upstairs and shower your booze away..."

*

Much much later, the front door slammed and Maddy marched in, Joey trudging along meekly behind her.

"What's wrong?" I asked.

Maddy slammed her bag down. "Angelica is a sell-out! And so is Genie Stacie!"

Now *there* was good news if I ever heard it.

"What happened?" Julian asked as Joey sat down opposite us, Maddy leaning on her armrest.

"Genie Stacie took us shopping. Then we stopped for a drink-" I raised my eyebrows at her- "Chill out, Mom, just a diet coke for Joey and me."

I looked at Joey who nodded. "I hate booze." Which was great news for me. At least it wasn't hereditary.

"I believe you. And then?" This was getting better and better by the second.

"And then these guys come up to us and ask us to take them to a club in Siena for a couple of hours. As if I had a couple of hours with *your* curfew. But that's not the point. Genie and Angelica looked at each other and just went, leaving me and Joey, her own daughter, there like two idiots. I mean, wasn't Genie supposed to stop *us* from going, being an adult and all, and not vice-versa?"

I sighed and shook my head, trying to hide my pure glee. So Genie wasn't so great after all.

"You girls did the right thing.," Julian said, then turned to Joey. "Sweetie, your mom is going through..."

But Joey sighed. "Julian, I really appreciate your concern for me, but you don't have to protect me. I know my mom is a flake."

I almost choked on my coffee.

"Mom?" Maddy said. "I mean, wouldn't you have told them to take a hike?"

"Uh, absolutely. Of course."

"So then why- forget it, I already know the answer. Mom?"

"Yeah?"

Maddy looked up into my face and grinned. "What's for dinner tonight?"

It would've been nice to say "Your favorite, Sweetie," but all I had was a kilogram of fava beans Renata had given me the day before and they were one thing Maddy didn't like.

"Tell you what. Why don't we order a pizza? We can have it on trays in front of the TV and just hang out, the four of us, what do you think?"

"Sounds good," she chimed and skipped off with Joey. Which was just as well as my eyes were starting to water.

I turned to Julian. "So I guess we won't be having that talk with Genie Stacie tonight, huh?"

Julian shook his head. "Doesn't look like it."

I heaved a sigh of relief.

*

Besides experiencing a mega-hangover the next morning, I experienced something just as surreal. My period was in its eighth day of absentia. Now *that* had never happened before. Could it be? I doubled-checked the date and performed an auto-diagnosis.

Breasts? Sore, but that had been a given lately.

Appetite? I could eat a horse. As usual.

Mood swings? Come on, you should know me by now.

Julian was sitting at his desk, his head in his hands. "Hey, honey, how are you feeling?" I asked and he looked up, his eyes unfocused. This Joey thing was taking its toll on him too, I realized. It wasn't about me and my hopes. The guy had just found out he could be a father to a girl he hardly knew.

Julian groaned. "I'm freaked out. Confused, Scared."

Welcome to my world, I wanted to say. But hell, for once it wasn't going to be about me.

"That smile, the teeth, the laugh. It's like looking at old school pictures- me with long hair."

I shrugged, determined to be helpful and selfless. "We'll do whatever it takes. It's not Joey's fault. Plus think of the shock on her when she finds out."

Julian sighed and nodded. "That's what really worries me. I've decided to postpone my book tour."

I looked up. "Oh?"

He shrugged. "As you said, I need to sort out the legalities pertaining to Joey. I want to tell her as soon as possible."

"Ok. Good idea."

"What did you want to tell me before?" Julian asked, wiping his forehead.

I frowned at him.

"When you came in."

"Uh, nothing. I just came in to see if you wanted a cup of tea." If I hadn't been hung over I would've reached for the whisky instead.

*

No one was ever allowed behind Julian's door. We all knew that. Yet, there he was with Genie Stacie, presumably having The Talk.

"Jules, lots of men that haven't got the guts to leave their wives can still be perfectly happy with another woman. And besides, you always told me I'm the love of your life."

I swallowed and almost grabbed the door to keep myself from swooning. *What...?* I didn't know *that!*

Julian was silent, and I could feel him debating through the two-inch oak wood door. Oh God, was he really going to do it? Was he really going to leave me after all these years now that his life-time love had reappeared like an H-bomb in our home?

Another sigh, almost a hushed moan.

I buried my head in my hands. Was my husband in Genie Stacie's arms, letting her kiss his doubts away? I wanted to barge in on them and shriek a long-pent-up, "Aha! I knew you were up to no good!" or something similar, but my stomach gave a lurch I thought I'd be sick in the corridor. That would not earn me any brownie points in case he was still debating, teetering over the brink between *Genie-Stacie, love of my life since I can remember and did I mention mother of my child* and… what's her name again? Oh yeah- *Erica, the neurotic, unstable and manic wife of eight years whom I constantly have to reassure and who, by the way, hasn't given me a child yet.*

No contest.

Silence again. Then, a kissing sound. My heart lurched. "Come back home with me, Jules. Please. I'll even produce your movie for you- star in it for free- anything you want. I miss you…"

It was practically a done deal. No man would turn down the chance to be with his biological daughter in a Hollywood mansion while his movie was being funded by his lover. The movie was what Julian desired more than life itself. And Genie Stacie's presence would make sure it raked in the big bucks.

"I'll give you until tomorrow morning to think it over. And then I'm calling my lawyer. What I tell him is your decision. It's in your hands, Jules."

And then just like that, the door opened and Genie Stacie sashayed out, sending me a satisfied smirk. I ducked my head through the door.

"Julian?" I whispered, my eyes moist. It had been a while.

Julian got to his feet and began to pace,

"What are you going to do?"

"I've no choice. I'm going to follow Genie Stacie and Josephine back to The States and get myself a damn good lawyer. I can't not see my daughter, Erica."

Of course I understood. I'd have done the same. Little did I know it was the beginning of the end of us.

CHAPTER TWENTY-ONE: Going Global

The days dragged by. My only contacts with the world were my friends, particularly Paul and Renata, my life-lines.

"Don't take it out on him, Erica," Paul said over the phone. Was it a coincidence that the important men in my life were all in the States? Julian, my Dad, Julian, Paul, my brother, his sons. "What's done is done."

"I keep telling myself that. I know he didn't cheat on me, and I swear to you I love Joey."

"I know you do. She sounds adorable. Just think of how she'll benefit from all this. A stable family- a step-mom who can actually cook!"

I smiled. "Step-mom. Does that sound okay? I keep thinking of bloody Cinderella."

Paul chuckled. "You'll do fine. You've always been so full of love. And right now Julian needs you more than anything."

"I know."

"Then why do you need me to tell you?"

"Because I miss you, Paulie. When are you coming back?"

"As soon as I finish this rich bitch's wedding in Phoenix, I'm all yours."

"I want to have a special lunch for Joey when they get back. Introduce her to the townspeople. If she'll be living here I want her to feel at home."

"She's already home with you guys, Erica."

"Thanks, Paulie…"

I thought about it. Paul was right. It was amazing the clarity that derived from sharing a problem with a loved one. Paul was such a scatter-brain in his own love-life, but in mine he saw everything crystal clear. Julian and I would be Joey's rock. Together, Julian and I would face it all.

*

"Honey, are you okay?" came my sister's voice over the phone all the way from Boston. And it wasn't even one a.m. yet.

As if. "Yes, Why?" She couldn't already know. I hadn't told anyone in the family.

"You don't watch your satellite TV much, huh? Do yourself a favor and turn it on, will you?"

"What channel?"

"Any channel. It's all over the news."

"Is it Julian? Is he okay?" I rasped as my heart jumped into my throat. Just as we were slowly trying to piece our lives back together again…

I gripped the phone in naked terror, already seeing myself standing in a horrible black dress in a graveyard. Julian had left for his umpteenth trip to the States yesterday. Had his plane crashed? Was I an unwitting widow? Had he been caught in a tsunami? An earthquake? Had someone kidnapped him? Had a bomb dropped on his hotel? Had my nightmares somehow come true after all?

"Oh, he's fine- at least until *you* get your hands on him," my sister snorted angrily as I fumbled with the remote. I was so nervous I dropped it twice. And, practically on every channel, there he was, my beautiful husband, with his arms around Genie Stacie as he practically pushed her into a limousine, so desperate was he to get his hands on her- so desperate was he to touch a thin, beautiful and glamorous woman again.

"The tabloids and media have described their secret night out like a Homecoming," Judy informed me. "And they even have a kid together? When were you going to tell me?"

But I was unable to think, unable to even dislike her sick joke. My brain was like frozen and my face paralyzed.

He was going to try to *reason* with Genie Stacie to see Joey- not roll around in a limousine with her! How could he *do* this to me, go parading around the world, now flaunting his once presumably clandestine relationship even in front of *cameras*? How did he think he was going to get away with it this time? Unless, of course, he didn't care anymore. He was done. Genie Stacie and his biological daughter were his final choice, and he hadn't even bothered to let me know.

I could've taken anything from anybody, but not this. Not Julian- the man I had trusted enough to try marriage again. The only one who I thought would never hurt me, had done it in one single blow.

"Erica, are you there? Don't be upset, honey- men are all the same. Why don't I fly over we can sit this one out together? We'll go shopping and spend all our husbands' money, ok?"

Truth was I had been wrong to be so sure of Julian. I'd given him my full support regarding Joey. All he had to do was go get himself a lawyer, go through a few hearings and get at least joint-custody. Easy. But no, men have to be men. Cheaters. Liars. Dedicated to their own pleasures. Forget the wife and kids. People should be *incarcerated* for cheating. Really, why is it that they go unpunished?

I could have called Julian (just to tell him what I thought of him) but he beat me to it.

"I'm busy," I snapped at Maddy who was holding the phone to me.

She eyed me, up to my elbows in the kitchen sink, with a look halfway between contempt and pity. My daughter's idol had finally managed to take my husband back.

"Mom- you want my advice? Talk to him. You don't want to upset him. Anger is not *sexy*."

What the hell did she know about sexy? What did *I* know about sexy?"

I'd had enough of people telling me I didn't want to piss off the man that had lowered himself to marry a mere mortal like me and then wanted out the minute his starlet appeared. Julian was *not* perfect. Far from it. When were people going to understand that and stop venerating him like a bloody god? It was more than obvious. But only to me. He cheated on me and *I* had to talk to *him*?

"Is he still there?" I asked her, then took the phone from her. "Are you still there?" I repeated to him.

"I'm here, sweetheart," came his deep, low voice. The voice of the man I loved more than any other and who had betrayed me at the drop of a hat.

"Good," I said. And hung up on him.

Maddy stared at me, shaking her head, "Don't say I didn't tell you."

When Renata came over I shook my head before she even opened her mouth. "I don't want to hear it."

"Hear what?" she said as she sat down, fanning herself from the heat.

"This is all your fault! If I hadn't listened to you I wouldn't be in this mess!"

She stared at me. "What the hell are you talking about?"

So I filled her in. About Josephine, Genie Stacie's attempts to steal him and finally how she succeeded.

"Don't be silly- Julian loves you, not her."

"Really? Then take a look this!" I hollered, flicking the remote to the entertainment channel. And, as if on cue, there they were, Julian and Genie Stacie, his hands on her Brazilian Butt as he pushed her into a limo. The speaker's voice rambled on and on about how Julian Foxham, formerly of the Redsox, had reunited with his one and only love, without even informing his wife, an Italian *lodger*.

Renata watched for a bit, then looked at me.

"There must be an explanation," she said finally.

"Yeah- my husband is in love with another woman who has given him what he wanted most- a daughter."

"You're not even going to listen to his explanation?"

"Would you?"

"Marco doesn't know any models."

"I'm serious!"

"Oh, Erica- really. You're going to listen to this garbage?"

"There," I said, flicking the remote. "The volume is off. The sight of my husband's hands on Genie Stacie's Brazilian butt is enough."

Renata rolled her eyes. "Stop it. When he gets home you'll get a perfectly logical explanation."

Paul called Maddy's cell phone to reach me as mine was permanently off now. I grabbed it like a lifeline and dashed upstairs.

"Sunshine…" was all he said and I melted. He was the only man who would never break my heart.

"Paulie- this is the end…" I sobbed in the privacy of the Master bedroom. To think that Julian wouldn't be sleeping here with me ever again was breaking my heart. To think that he'd deliberately thrown us away.

"Don't be silly. There's a perfectly good explanation."

"That's exactly what Renata said, but I don't believe it."

"Julian called me. He says you won't talk to him."

My heart lurched. "What did he say?"

"That the media flipped it upside down completely."

"Really…"

"Don't be like that. He says that they had a huge fight and she tried to kill herself with barbiturates. He was simply bringing her to the hospital."

"Huh…" was all I could say. Paul had always partial to Julian, to put it mildly, calling him *The Man of Our Life*.

He groaned. "Jesus, Sunshine- don't you remember all that he's done for you, Erica? Don't you remember how he was there for you after Ira left you?"

I swallowed. Of course I did. Julian had restored my faith in myself. And in love.

"And don't you remember how he broke into your home to save your life when Ira attacked you with that baseball bat?"

I remembered.

"And don't you remember how he stayed with you and the kids all night after that?"

And the time he carried me home when I had showed up at his office after dark, having walked for miles, blisters on my feet. And the time Ira kidnapped Maddy, how he stayed with me all night. And the time when I showed up on his doorstep in the middle of the night and we… yeah. I remembered it all. I remembered every single word, every single caress that had sent me to heaven and back. I remembered how even his name could make me tingle all over with excitement.

But now things were different. Now I couldn't trust him anymore and that was that. Eight years, I'd loved this man. With all my heart, believing that not all men were like my first husband Ira. As it turned out, I was wrong.

*

Two days and two nights of not sleeping later, while I was conjuring up many scenarios, Julian came through the front door, absolutely drained. He was the last person I wanted to see and the last thing I wanted to hear were his lies about why he had his hands on Genie Stacie's butt.

"Hi," he said tiredly, hesitating on the threshold as if I'd booby-trapped it. Eight years and my bedroom was once again iffy territory. I couldn't believe I was back here again. I'd had my fill of Ira and deceiving men, but this? This took the proverbial cake.

"We need to talk," he said as he put his bag down.

I gave him my world-famous hairy eyeball and then turned away. Talk? We were past that. *So* past it.

Damn, if only none of this had happened, we'd be hugging and kissing. Never again. I swiped at my eyes. "I'm not interested, Julian."

He reached out and took my arm. I looked down at his hand coolly, so composed. I'd die before I let him know how that footage had made me suffer.

"Do you mind?" I asked.

He let go, but I knew he was dying to slam me down onto a chair and read me the riot act. As if *I*'d been the one away playing with an old flame.

"I think you and I need to discuss a few things."

"There's nothing to discuss, Julian. Can you let me through to the kitchen now? I have to cook my family dinner."

"Genie Stacie and I had a huge fight. She then went out drinking. What was I supposed to do, leave her drunk in the middle of the road? I am the father of her child after all. I couldn't let Joey think I didn't care.

"So you decided to go pick her up with a limousine?"

"It was the hotel car…"

"And you had to put your hands on her butt?"

"I was trying to get her into the car, she was putting up a fight…."

"I don't believe you anymore. You've lied to me too many times."

He looked at me, his eyes red. Whether from fatigue or tears, I didn't know. "I forgave you for Alberto…" he whispered. "I believed you. Why can't you believe me?"

Alberto again. But that had been just one kiss. This was a love-child. "Because this is not the same."

Julian groaned and sat down on the bed. I ignored him and left to sleep in the guest bedroom. There was no way I could sleep with him by my side tonight- or ever again. Not with this hanging between us. This was something that wasn't going away.

CHAPTER TWENTY-TWO: Tempus and Husbands Fugit

Before I knew it, the summer was over and with it all my hopes of motherhood and a happy marriage. Maddy was back at school and Warren was attending his new courses at university in Siena.

Julian and I were barely talking as he was flying to and fro from the States on a regular basis, this time to tape an interview in San Francisco, leaving me alone yet again in our great big house. Because now how I felt was of no consequence to him. He'd tried to talk to me, but it was as if he wasn't even there. To me, he'd left me long before that. Not only did he not care how I felt, he did nothing to alleviate my pain.

We were officially over. It only remained for one of us to actually come out and say it. He came and went, leaving me messages that I never bothered to read. Let him go to New York, L.A. Let him go anywhere he wanted. I didn't need to know how he and Genie Stacie were facing parenthood together.

I only felt bad because Joey had no fault. I wanted to see her, mother her, but there was nothing I could do. Maybe I could write her a letter. Explain that none of my feelings for her had changed. But Genie Stacie would only tear it up or convince Joey I was lying. It was a false world, Hollywood.

The phone call came out of the blue. At first I didn't recognize the muffled moan and thought of a crank call.

"Erica- it's Judy..."

"Judy, what's up?"

"Erica, you have to come home..."

My heart shrank to the size of a marble. "What's wrong?"

"It's Dad... he died this morning."

*

One phone call and Renata was there, kids in tow, as I threw a few things into an overnight case, not sure what I was doing or how long I'd be staying.

I swiped at my eyes, refusing to fall apart. *Passport. Toothbrush. Cell-phone, even if it didn't work in the US. Wallet.*

"When did it happen?" Renata asked as she passed me random things and I lobbed them into my bag.

"This morning. I have to go, I have to go. Judy and Vince don't do well in emergencies."

Renata put a hand on my shoulder.

Dad. Dear, dear old Dad…

It was a three-flight ordeal; Siena-Milan, Milan-New York, New York-Boston, for a total of fifteen hours including the stop-overs.

I don't even remember boarding the Milan-New York flight, but as I sat there all strapped in, staring over the sea of heads in front of me, an elderly couple kept turning to look at me worriedly. I must have looked like a real mess. Maybe they even thought I was a terrorist debating at the last moment whether to go ahead with my kamikaze mission.

I giggled and pulled out my compact mirror. Nothing new in there, except that I didn't recognize me at all. If I had never been a dead ringer for Angelina Jolie, the woman in my mirror looked like an overstuffed scarecrow with deep-sunken eyes.

How had this happened so suddenly? I should've seen the signs. And then I remembered I had. Marcy had been driving dad crazy for years.

"It's never as bad as it seems," came a soft, strangled voice. I opened my eyes and found a kind, wrinkly face only inches from my own.

"Love comes and goes. The only problem that can't be dealt with is death."

I stared at the old woman, but because she had absolutely no idea of what she was talking about, I smiled kindly, although on the inside I was screaming. Right now Julian and Genie Stacie were the least of my problems.

*

As the Jews who roamed the land for forty years, so did I the New York terminal looking for my connection, but all the letters on the screen made me so dizzy I thought I would collapse from sheer exhaustion. My mouth felt like someone had forced a bale of hay down my throat and my head felt like someone had been bashing my brains in.

"Erica?"

I whirled around and, after a moment of ultra-shock added to my already existing shock, focused on the familiar face.

"Ira," I breathed. He looked terrible.

"Erica- you look amazing."

Years of doing my best and he never noticed and now that I looked like shit he comes out and compliments me.

"You're about nine years late," I said and his brow shot up into hi non-existent hairline. All his hair was, in fact gone. He was scrawny with a huge belly. He looked at least two feet shorter.

"What?"

"Nothing," I said hastily. "Where are you going?"

"Atlantic City. I'm waiting for... some buddies of mine."

Yeah, right.

"And you? I heard you were in Italy."

He'd *heard* it from my lawyer regarding Julian's request to adopt Maddy and Warren seven years ago. But all that didn't matter anymore.

"My dad just died. I'm going home for the funeral."

We both turned at the sound of a shrill voice- a (would you believe it?) Genie Stacie look alike.

He looked at her, his eyes wide with lust, then back at me.

The last thing I needed was to meet another one of Ira's lovers. "That's my flight," I said. "Gotta go."

He nodded, his eyes unfocused, as if he'd been drinking or smoking dope. "Say hi to your parents for me." And with that, he turned to face the blonde running to him. She wasn't a day over twenty.

Say hi to my parents? He hadn't even been listening to me. Twelve whole years of my life spent trying to get *this* guy to love me. And he hadn't even asked about his own children. Children that Julian had lovingly taken on board.

There was no one like Julian.

I swallowed back the bitter knot in my throat as I ran for my gate, the babelic cacophony just about to make my head explode.

*

As we touched down at Logan International, I had a strong déjà vu of Julian, the kids and I flying out of Boston for a new life only eight years ago. Not a long time, really, but if you stop and think of how many things can change in eight years.

Julian and I had built a business from scratch. We belonged to a friendly Italian community and loved every brick and pan tile of Castellino. We were a team. Well, we *had been*. I searched my memory, every nook and cranny of it, for signs that things had started to go wrong. When had he fallen out of love with me? And when had he fallen out of love with life in Italy? What had made him crack- the lazy bums at the post office, the endless bureaucracy, the slow pace of life when all he wanted to do was fly, fly, fly?

And most importantly, had Genie Stacie's arrival only accelerated our destiny? Was he going to leave eventually anyway? What could I have done to prevent it?

Even now- I'd supported him throughout his new-found fatherhood. Been right behind him every step of the way. A lesser woman would've ditched him there and then. But I'd loved him. He'd been my everything. And now that I needed him most, he'd turned on me.

*

Paul came to pick me up at the airport along with Judy's eldest son Tony who gave me the full details of how grandpa had *keeled over* after yet *another* argument with Grandma. Last month it was her Visa bills, two months ago her cell-phone bill.

Paul glanced over at me. He was always there when I needed him. "You holding together, sunshine?" he whispered and I nodded although I was about to fall apart any minute.

I couldn't believe I was here, after all these years, in this traffic that seemed like a revved up, out of control movie reel where nothing made sense. I had lived a whole lifetime in Italy in the meantime, but funnily, at the same time it was as if I'd never left. Paul was here, Tony was here. Soon I'd see my aunts Maria, Martina and Monica, my sister Judy, my brother Vince and Sandra, Marcy- the whole bunch. Except for (I swallowed back the pain) my father.

Dad was gone, all of a sudden, bringing me back to where my home had been, among my family members. I was catapulted years back, to when I was a kid and my Nonna Silvia had died.

Back home in Italy, Renata would make sure the kids weren't alone. I missed Julian terribly. Right in my chest there was a huge Julian-shaped hole that only he could fit. But what was the point of calling him? We were no longer an item. That was the long and short of it. We had reached the end of the line. Besides, even if he was here, what could he say besides the platitudes that I simply couldn't bear at the moment?

"...you know, aunt Erica?"

"Uh-huh." I leaned forward to the driver's seat. "Paul, I love you but can you please slow down? My Dad's dead, he's not going anywhere."

Paul nodded but my nephew cast me a side-long glance and his lip began to tremble. Shit. The kid really loved the old man. And now that he was gone I struggled to wonder how things were going to be different without him.

"Don't cry, Aunt Erica," Tony said and as we pulled up in front of my parents' house, I began to panic.

I can't remember how I made my way through the front door. I barely remember the coffin, the teary faces of distant relatives I'd only seen two or three times in my life. All I remember is my aunts Maria, Martina and Monica embracing me, enveloping me with their familiar support, and somehow the panic subsided.

"That's our girl," Zia Maria soothed as Zia Martina nodded and Zia Monica dried her eyes. "Everything's going to be alright."

I nodded in return, straightened my back and took a deep breath. They had reminded me about my strength so that I could be strong for Marcy and my siblings.

Marcy reached out to kiss me in a gesture of unusual selflessness. "Poor Erica, what a shock for you," she sobbed into my coat, and my arms automatically went around her shoulders.

I shook hands with people, let them hang onto me, hold me, caress my cheek, while all the time I was wondering if Maddy had done her homework, if Warren used a condom with his new girlfriend, how Renata was coping, and if our dog Susie missed me. My body was there, but my mind was in Italy. And my heart, as they say, in San Francisco.

Julian had given me the chance to believe in a fresh start. To believe in myself, and that not all was so bad. But I hadn't come such a long way if now I couldn't even manage to pick up the phone and tell him my father had died.

I detached myself from the throng and went up to my old room to make the call. There was nothing left of mine in there except for my old phone and my dear, old record player. It looked sort of rusty, as if it would fall apart if I dared to push a button.

With a loud sigh I dialed Julian's number and listened to three rings, then his phone conked out.

After that I called home. Maddy answered and I could hear Susie barking outside through the open door. It must have been yet another beautiful day in Italy.

"Pronto?" my daughter said in perfect Italian, although her voice was low and sad.

"Maddy, it's me."

I heard her breath intake before she said, "Mom! Finally- how are you?" and I wanted to cry at the new-found tenderness in her voice.

"Fine, fine. I'm at Grandma's."

"Oh, Mom, I'm so so sorry..." she whispered.

"I know, thank you, sweetie..."

"How is Grandma taking it? Please give her a hug for me, will you?"

"I will, Maddy. Did you tell Warren yet?"

"I did and he wants to come back but he has an exam tomorrow so I said there was no point and that I'd keep him posted."

"That's good, sweetie. Thank you."

"Renata is here, she wants to talk to you. And Mom...? Hang in there, ok?"

"I will," I whispered feeling guilty and at the same time elated I would be going home soon.

There were muffled words and then Renata came on. "Erica, sweetheart. How are you?"

"I'm fine." *My dad's the dead one,* I almost said, but luckily stopped myself in time. I'd already freaked the family out with my flippancy.

"We've sent a telegram- everyone in Castellino has. Maddy found the address."

"Thank you, everybody."

And that was all I could muster for that day.

The next day, as I ducked into the family limousine that would take us to the funeral hall I glanced up as a taxi pulled up next to me. The door opened and out came Julian in a black coat, a somber expression on his face.

There was a murmur to the effect that, *See? She's not divorcing- there's her husband now.*

He stopped right in front of me, his eyes searching mine.

"You look absolutely gorgeous," was all I could say as Julian folded me in his arms, instantly filling me with that usual warmth that could only come from him.

"I'm so sorry, sweetheart," he breathed into my hair. "Maddy called me. I took the first flight back, why didn't you tell me..." Or that's what I think he said.

Then he turned to Marcy and embraced her. She clung to him and started to cry really hard, her nose going red and dripping.

Then came Judy who threw herself at him so violently he almost dropped her. "Oh, Julian, you came..." she breathed like Scarlett O'Hara and started to cry. Vince pried her out of Julian's arms and shook his hand thoroughly. Vince had always liked Julian. Everybody had always liked him. Because he was a decent guy, and my beef with him would have to wait for a better time.

For now he was here, and that was enough.

CHAPTER TWENTY-TWO: The Beginning

It was cold for late December and the trees surrounding the cemetery were like giant burning black arrows shooting up into an anthrax sky.

We had buried my dad three days earlier and at my request to return to the cemetery Judy insisted on accompanying me and Julian while Vince stayed home with Marcy. I wanted to share with my husband one of the most important things in my life.

Winter was already a fact and I breathed in the familiar fragrance of Boston just before a snowfall.

I slung my arm through Julian's and stuffed my free hand into the new black coat I'd purchased at- you guessed it- Macy's (without Marcy) and headed towards the South side of the cemetery.

"Dad's grave is the other way," Judy called after us. I stopped amidst the flaming leaves, kicking at them with my feet the way I used to as a girl.

"I'm not going to Dad's grave right now," I called back, and to Julian who was regarding me quizzically, I smiled and explained, "I'm taking you to meet my Grandma Silvia."

We stopped just before her headstone. *Silvia Bettarini, Beloved Mother and Grandmother.*

"You'd have loved her. She was amazing."

"She was if she was anything like you."

I turned to look at him and our eyes held as he pulled me close for a kiss and I fell against him. I hadn't done that in a long time.

"Erica- you are amazing. You always have been. I love you so much, sweetheart."

"I love you too, Julian…"

"When we get home we'll take the kids on a fantastic trip- anywhere you want."

"Anywhere?"

"Absolutely."

I smiled as a snowflake landed on my nose and Julian kissed it.

*

It was only on the flight back, on Julian's shoulder, that I finally allowed myself to cry. Really cry.

Sweet, mild Dad. Never a harsh word, never a reproach. Just his mild smiles and weak words of compliance. "Yes, Marcy. No, Marcy."

And now none of it mattered anymore. I was only sorry that he wouldn't get to meet the two new additions to the family. Joey… and… well… it had been at least six weeks since my period.

I'd done a pregnancy test in Marcy's en-suite bathroom, my hands shaking so badly I had to repeat it three times. How ironic, I'd asked myself, that I'm pregnant now that Julian and I are over?

Yet I couldn't bring myself to tell Julian just yet because I was afraid that he- I knew it would be a boy- might go away.

Outside Siena airport at the end of a long journey home, Julian wrapped his arms around me and I hugged him back hard as he opened the door of his Jeep for me.

I turned to look up at him, feeling my mouth widen with a big smile.

"What?" Julian said, somewhat thrown. We'd just come back from my Dad's funeral and somehow I couldn't stop the feeling of hope and life that was now bursting inside me once we'd arrived on home soil. "What's funny?"

"I'll tell you when we get home."

"Give me a hint at least."

"Well, let's say I've got a nice Christmas present."

I wanted to tell him when we were home. And together we would tell our kids Maddy, Warren and Joey. But first, we had to have The Reveal talk with Joey who still had no idea she was Julian's daughter.

*

"Joey, sweetie, Erica and I have to tell you something," Julian said softly.

"I know," she answered just as quietly. "You're my father."

Julian and I stared at each other, then back at her.

"I've known for a long time," she confessed, and again our eyes swung to each other's. "But I just couldn't write you and tell you. I didn't want to ruin your life."

Julian's mouth dropped open. "Ruin my- sweetheart, how could you ruin my life? You are an amazing girl, and any man would be thrilled to have you as a daughter."

Joey stayed with us and enrolled in the International University for Foreigners in nearby Perugia. She'd had the choice between living in Perugia or commuting, as it was only fifty kilometers away, but he chose to be with us, her family- something she'd always craved for.

Maddy was in her fourth year of the Academy of Art and had buckled down for her assignments. She and Angelica were as close as ever, and together with Joey, they formed a trio we dubbed Charlie's Angels because there was a blonde, a brunette and a redhead. Well, Julian dubbed them. I thought it was corny but then again, when don't I?

Warren was in his third year of Medicine and sad to have lost his grandfather, but at the same time overjoyed to have gained a sister who was a baseball freak like him. He was also grateful to have escaped teenage fatherhood. He still dated but was always, he says, very careful.

As far as my sweet secret was concerned, I was saving it for the next day, Christmas Eve, the very same day my children had lost a member of their family, Ira, for the first time. Tomorrow night I'd sit them all around the tree and announce that the family was getting bigger. Four children. And a loving husband. How lucky could I get?

EPILOGUE

Ciao, *bella*, want arride?" came the deep voice at my side as I trudged up the dirt road leading to our home with my eternally flat tire. Men. They never stop trying.

"You shouldn't be bicycling around in your state, you stubborn American woman," he grinned wickedly as he lifted my bike into the back of his car and placed his hands on my hips, very intimate and sure of himself.

Sure, he was sexy as hell, but what made him think I was going to surrender to him in the middle of a country road as the pale, February sun set behind a Tuscan hill? Just because he smelled so great and I knew for a fact he was a really good lover?

"How about you come back to my place, *si*? I'll give you a long, long massage," Julian drawled, nuzzling my neck.

Any more romantic and I wouldn't have felt married to the guy.

THE END

APOLOGY

As much as I wish it were real, Castellino is a fictitious town of my own making that sums up everything I love about Tuscany, my home for six years and where my best friends still live today.

Visit www.nancybarone.com and Pinterest for photos and recipes from this glorious Italian region. And by all means, leave one of your own. We love to eat in Italy!

Visit Nancy's website:

www.nancybarone.com

*

If you like Paranormal Romance, check out my naughtier side with Rowyn Ashby's books.

Inside Out (Etopia Press)

Sicilian Heat (Etopia Press)

Printed in Great Britain
by Amazon